Acting Edition

M000112875

Rodgers & Hammerstein's
Cinderella
(Enchanted Edition)

Music by
Richard Rodgers

Book and Lyrics by
Oscar Hammerstein II

Adapted for the stage by
Tom Briggs

From the teleplay by
Robert L. Freedman

CONCORD
THEATRICALS

Book Copyright © 2009 by the Family Trust u/w Richard Rodgers and Hammerstein Properties, LLC.

Original Book Copyright © 1957, 1985 by Richard Rodgers and Oscar Hammerstein II, and by the Estate of Richard Rodgers and the Estate of Oscar Hammerstein II. Copyright Renewed. International Copyright Secured.

All Rights Reserved

CINDERELLA is fully protected under the copyright laws of the United States of America, the British Commonwealth, including Canada, and all member countries of the Berne Convention for the Protection of Literary and Artistic Works, the Universal Copyright Convention, and/or the World Trade Organization conforming to the Agreement on Trade Related Aspects of Intellectual Property Rights. All rights, including professional and amateur stage productions, recitation, lecturing, public reading, motion picture, radio broadcasting, television, online/digital production, and the rights of translation into foreign languages are strictly reserved.

ISBN 78-0-573-70889-3

www.concordtheatricals.com
www.concordtheatricals.co.uk

FOR PRODUCTION INQUIRIES

UNITED STATES AND CANADA
info@concordtheatricals.com
1-866-979-0447

UNITED KINGDOM AND EUROPE
licensing@concordtheatricals.co.uk
020-7054-7298

Each title is subject to availability from Concord Theatricals Corp., depending upon country of performance. Please be aware that CINDERELLA may not be licensed by Concord Theatricals Corp. in your territory. Professional and amateur producers should contact the nearest Concord Theatricals Corp. office or licensing partner to verify availability.

CAUTION: Professional and amateur producers are hereby warned that CINDERELLA is subject to a licensing fee. The purchase, renting, lending or use of this book does not constitute a license to perform this title(s), which license must be obtained from Concord Theatricals Corp. prior to any performance. Performance of this title(s) without a license is a violation of federal law and may subject the producer and/or presenter of such performances to civil penalties. Both amateurs and professionals considering a production are strongly advised to apply to the appropriate agent before starting rehearsals, advertising, or booking a theatre. A licensing fee must be paid whether the title(s) is presented for charity or gain and whether or not admission is charged. Professional/Stock licensing fees are quoted upon application to Concord Theatricals Corp.

This work is published by R&H Theatricals, an imprint of Concord Theatricals Corp.

No one shall make any changes in this title(s) for the purpose of production. No part of this book may be reproduced, stored in a retrieval system, scanned, uploaded, or transmitted in any form, by any means, now known or yet to be invented, including mechanical, electronic, digital, photocopying, recording, videotaping, or otherwise, without the prior written permission of the publisher. No one shall share this title(s), or any part of this title(s), through any social media or file hosting websites.

For all inquiries regarding motion picture, television, online/digital and other media rights, please contact Concord Theatricals Corp.

THIRD-PARTY MATERIALS USE NOTE

Licensees are solely responsible for obtaining formal written permission from copyright owners to use copyrighted third-party materials (e.g., incidental music not provided in connection with a performance license, artworks, logos) in the performance of this play and are strongly cautioned to do so. If no such permission is obtained by the licensee, then the licensee must use only original materials and materials that the licensee owns and controls. Licensees are solely responsible and liable for clearances of all third-party copyrighted materials, and shall indemnify the copyright owners of the play(s) and their licensing agent, Concord Theatricals Corp., against any costs, expenses, losses and liabilities arising from the use of such copyrighted third-party materials by licensees. For music, please contact the appropriate music licensing authority in your territory for the rights to any incidental music not provided in connection with a performance license.

IMPORTANT BILLING AND CREDIT REQUIREMENTS

If you have obtained performance rights to this title, please refer to your licensing agreement for important billing and credit requirements.

ADDITIONAL COPYRIGHT INFORMATION

"The Prince Is Giving A Ball!" Copyright © 1957 by Richard Rodgers and Oscar Hammerstein II. Copyright Renewed. Additional lyrics by Fred Ebb. Copyright © 1998 by the Family Trust u/w Richard Rodgers, the Family Trust u/w Dorothy F. Rodgers, the Estate of Oscar Hammerstein II. Publishing and allied rights administered by Williamson Music, throughout the world. International Copyright Secured. All Rights Reserved. "In My Own Little Corner" Copyright © 1957 by Richard Rodgers and Oscar Hammerstein II. Copyright Renewed. "Godmother's Song (Fol-De-Rol)" Copyright © 1957 by Richard Rodgers and Oscar Hammerstein II. Copyright Renewed. "Impossible" Copyright © 1957 by Richard Rodgers and Oscar Hammerstein II. Copyright Renewed. "Ten Minutes Ago" Copyright © 1957 by Richard Rodgers and Oscar Hammerstein II. Copyright Renewed. "Stepsisters' Lament" Copyright © 1957 by Richard Rodgers and Oscar Hammerstein II. Copyright Renewed. "Do I Love You Because You're Beautiful?" Copyright © 1957 by Richard Rodgers and Oscar Hammerstein II. Copyright Renewed. "When You're Driving Through The Moonlight" Copyright © 1962 by Richard Rodgers and Dorothy Hammerstein, William Hammerstein, and Howard E. Reinheimer, as Executors of Oscar Hammerstein II. "A Lovely Night" Copyright © 1957 by Richard Rodgers and Oscar Hammerstein II. Copyright Renewed. "Boys And Girls Like You And Me" Copyright © 1943 (Copyright Renewed) and 1997 by Williamson Music. "The Sweetest Sounds" Copyright © 1962 by Richard Rodgers. Copyright Renewed. "Loneliness Of Evening" Copyright © 1949 by Richard Rodgers and Oscar Hammerstein II. Copyright Renewed. "There's Music In You" Copyright © 1952 by Richard Rodgers and Oscar Hammerstein II. Copyright Renewed. All Rights Reserved.

RODGERS & HAMMERSTEIN'S CINDERELLA premiered as a live television special starring Julie Andrews. The March 31, 1957 broadcast was viewed by more people than any other program in the history of television. In 1965, a new telecast starring Lesley Ann Warren was equally successful in transporting a new generation to the miraculous kingdom of Dreams Come True. In 1997, the musical returned to television in a star-studded presentation featuring Brandy as Cinderella and Whitney Houston as her Fairy Godmother. *CINDERELLA (ENCHANTED EDITION)* is inspired by that production.

CHARACTERS

CINDERELLA

FAIRY GODMOTHER

STEPMOTHER

GRACE – Cinderella's awkward stepsister

JOY – Cinderella's sullen stepsister

CHRISTOPHER – a charming young prince

LIONEL – his royal steward

QUEEN CONSTANTINA – his mother

KING MAXIMILLIAN – his father

CHARLES – a cat who will become a coachman

4 WHITE MICE – who will become horses

A DOVE – who will become a footman

VILLAGERS, MERCHANTS, MAIDENS, AND PALACE GUESTS

SETTING

The action takes place once upon a time in a kingdom far away.

INCLUSION STATEMENT

In this show, the race of the characters is not pivotal to the plot. We encourage you to consider diversity and inclusion in your casting choices.

MUSICAL NUMBERS

ACT I

"Prologue" . . . . Fairy Godmother,
Cinderella, Ensemble

"The Sweetest Sounds" . . . . Cinderella & Christopher

"The Prince Is Giving A Ball" . . . . Lionel, Stepfamily,
Cinderella, Villagers

"In My Own Little Corner" . . . . Cinderella & Animals

"Boys And Girls Like You And Me" . . . . King & Queen

"The Sweetest Sounds (Reprise)" . . . . Christopher
& Cinderella

"In My Own Little Corner (Reprise)" . . . . Cinderella

"Fol-De-Rol" . . . . Fairy Godmother

"Impossible" . . . . Fairy Godmother & Cinderella

"The Transformation" . . . . Fairy Godmother,
Cinderella, Animals

"It's Possible: Finale Act I" . . . . Cinderella, Fairy Godmother,
Horses, Coachman, Footman

ACT II

"Gavotte" . . . . Christopher, Maidens, Guests

"Loneliness Of Evening" . . . . Christopher

"The Cinderella Waltz" . . . . Cinderella, Christopher, Guests

"Ten Minutes Ago" . . . . Christopher, Cinderella, Company

"Stepsisters' Lament" . . . . Grace & Joy

"Do I Love You Because You're Beautiful?" . . . . Christopher & Cinderella

"Do I Love You Because You're Beautiful? (Reprise)" . . . . . . Christopher,
King, Queen,
Cinderella

"When You're Driving Through The Moonlight" . . . . Cinderella,
Stepmother,
Grace, Joy

"A Lovely Night" . . . . Cinderella, Stepmother,
Grace, Joy, Animals

"A Lovely Night (Reprise)" . . . . Cinderella

"The Search" . . . . Lionel, Christopher, Maidens

"There's Music In You" . . . . Fairy Godmother & Company

PROLOGUE

[MUSIC NO. 01 "PROLOGUE"]

(The curtain rises on a modest pumpkin patch illuminated by a full moon. The FAIRY GODMOTHER appears in the moon.)

FAIRY GODMOTHER. Once upon a time in a kingdom far away,
There lived a lovely little girl who smiled throughout the day.

(CINDERELLA enters beneath the moon.)

Her name was Cinderella and there was no child more joyful in the land.
But then one day her mother died, and Cinderella's father took her hand.

(A small tree appears.)

"We will plant a tree," he said, "and when you're full of doubt and fear, bring your troubled heart beneath this tree and Mother will be here."
Several years had come and gone when Cinderella's father died.
The brokenhearted child ran to her mother's tree and cried and cried.

(CINDERELLA runs to the tree, kneels, and weeps as, in the distance, the ENSEMBLE sings a choral lament.)

Her tears fell down upon the earth and made the tree to grow, and to this day, when she is sad, both tree and Mother know.

NOW YOU CAN GO WHEREVER YOU WANT TO GO!

NOW YOU CAN DO WHATEVER YOU WANT TO DO!
NOW YOU CAN BE WHATEVER YOU WANT TO BE!

> *(She holds her hand out toward* **CINDERELLA**,
> *and a* **DOVE** *flies to the tree.* **CINDERELLA** *looks
> up at the* **DOVE**, *smiling with an unexpected
> sense of comfort. The music continues as the
> scene shifts to:)*

ACT I

Scene One
The Village Square

(The **VILLAGERS** *go merrily about their business in the bustling marketplace, where the merchants include a* **BUTCHER, CLOTH MERCHANT, CHEESE MERCHANT, BAKER, FLOWER GIRL,** *and* **FRUIT SELLER***. The music segues into:)*

[MUSIC NO. 01A "THE VILLAGE (CINDERELLA MARCH)"]

(To the tempo of a haughty march, the **STEPMOTHER** *enters from the butcher shop, followed by her daughters,* **GRACE** *and* **JOY***.)*

STEPMOTHER. Come along, girls. So Grace, the butcher certainly was chatty with *you* today.

GRACE. He had pork on sale.

JOY. Pork isn't all he was pitchin'.

STEPMOTHER. "The butcher's wife never goes hungry."

GRACE. I'd rather starve.

JOY. That'll be the day.

STEPMOTHER. *(Spotting a hat outside the millinery shop.)* Aaahhh! Will you just look at that hat! I simply must try it on.

> *(Looking toward the butcher shop impatiently.)*

Oh...where is that girl? How long can it take to wrap a salmon? Cinderella...!

> *(***CINDERELLA** *enters from the butcher shop, nearly obscured by the stack of packages*

3

she carries, including a salmon wrapped in butcher's paper.)

STEPMOTHER. Wait here while we finish our shopping.

CINDERELLA. Yes, Stepmother.

(The **STEPMOTHER** *exits into the shop.)*

GRACE. Have you ever seen a slower girl in your life?

JOY. Who are *you* callin' slow?

GRACE. Not you, stupid –

(Indicating **CINDERELLA.***)*

– her!

*(***GRACE** *exits.)*

JOY. Oh.

(Then, realizing.)

Hey! Who are *you* callin' stupid?

*(***JOY** *exits.* **CINDERELLA** *sets the packages down and takes in the village scene with the delighted wonder of a girl who doesn't get out much. Music out. A* **LITTLE GIRL** *nearby winds a music box, then opens it to release the tinkling music.)*

[MUSIC NO. 02 "THE SWEETEST SOUNDS"]

CINDERELLA.
THE SWEETEST SOUNDS I'LL EVER HEAR
ARE STILL INSIDE MY HEAD.
THE KINDEST WORDS I'LL EVER KNOW
ARE WAITING TO BE SAID.
THE MOST ENTRANCING SIGHT OF ALL
IS YET FOR ME TO SEE,
AND THE DEAREST LOVE IN ALL THE WORLD
IS WAITING SOMEWHERE FOR ME –
IS WAITING SOMEWHERE,
SOMEWHERE FOR ME.

*(***CHRISTOPHER** *enters across the square – the handsome young prince of the kingdom in*

*disguise as a commoner. He saunters down
the street, basking in his anonymity.)*

CHRISTOPHER.
THE SWEETEST SOUNDS I'LL EVER HEAR
ARE STILL INSIDE MY HEAD.
THE KINDEST WORDS I'LL EVER KNOW
ARE WAITING TO BE SAID.

THE MOST ENTRANCING SIGHT OF ALL
IS YET FOR ME TO SEE,
AND THE DEAREST LOVE IN ALL THE WORLD
IS WAITING SOMEWHERE FOR ME –
IS WAITING SOMEWHERE,
SOMEWHERE FOR ME.

(Music continues under. The **STEPMOTHER**
*emerges from the millinery shop with a
hatbox, which she foists at* **CINDERELLA**.
GRACE *follows, now sporting a preposterous
hat and pursued by the irate* **JOY**.)*

JOY. I saw it first!

GRACE. Did not!

JOY. Did so!

GRACE. Not!

JOY. So!

GRACE. *Not!*

STEPMOTHER. *So* much squabbling, girls! Remember:
"Restraint above all else." So Joy –

(Referring to the millinery shop.)

Master Boxhorn certainly gave *you* the hairy eyeball.

JOY. He's too short.

STEPMOTHER. What he lacks in height he makes up for in
cash.

JOY. But you always said, "No girl should marry for money."

STEPMOTHER. No. I said, "...for money *only*." Anyway, that
was when you were younger, dear.

> *(The* **STEPFAMILY** *exits. As* **CINDERELLA** *and* **CHRISTOPHER** *sing in a round, they are never aware of each other, even as their paths cross.)*

CINDERELLA & CHRISTOPHER.

> THE SWEETEST SOUNDS I'LL EVER HEAR
> ARE STILL INSIDE MY HEAD.
> THE KINDEST WORDS I'LL EVER KNOW
> ARE WAITING TO BE SAID.
>
> THE MOST ENTRANCING SIGHT OF ALL
> IS YET FOR ME TO SEE,
> AND THE DEAREST LOVE IN ALL THE WORLD
> IS WAITING SOMEWHERE FOR ME –
> IS WAITING SOMEWHERE...

CHRISTOPHER.

> ...SOMEWHERE FOR ME.

CINDERELLA. *(Picking up her packages.)*

> ...SOMEWHERE FOR ME.

CINDERELLA & CHRISTOPHER.

> WAITING SOMEWHERE...

> *(***CHRISTOPHER** *turns and accidentally bumps into* **CINDERELLA,** *knocking the packages from her arms. Music out.)*

CHRISTOPHER. Oh... Excuse me, miss. Are you all right? I'm so sorry. I...

> *(They kneel to retrieve the packages and come face-to-face – an enchanted moment as they really see each other for the first time.)*

Please, forgive me.

CINDERELLA. *(Mesmerized.)* I do.

> *(Suddenly self-conscious.)*

I mean...

> *(She nervously gathers her packages.)*

CHRISTOPHER. *(Helping collect the packages.)* What's your name?

CINDERELLA. What's yours?

CHRISTOPHER. You know, I really think names are overrated. I mean, what's in a name?

CINDERELLA. Exactly.

CHRISTOPHER. *(Handing her the stack of packages.)* Well, it was nice "bumping" into you.

CINDERELLA. You're very kind.

CHRISTOPHER. *(Placing a flower on her stack of packages.)* Everyone deserves to be treated with kindness and respect.

[MUSIC NO. 03 "THE PRINCE IS GIVING A BALL"]

(We hear a brass fanfare. LIONEL enters officiously, making his way through the square. He is Prince CHRISTOPHER's royal steward. CINDERELLA crosses out of his way.)

LIONEL. Gangway...comin' through...royal business...

CHRISTOPHER. Lionel...?! Yikes!

(He races to hide behind the butcher cart.)

LIONEL. Look lively...move it or lose it...

(He steps up onto the base of the fountain.)

Hear ye, hear ye! A royal proclamation! Hear ye all!

(Introduction music begins as CHRISTOPHER edges out from behind the cart, curious about LIONEL's proclamation.)

(To CHRISTOPHER.) This is gonna be of special interest to ye.

(CHRISTOPHER *recoils at the realization that* **LIONEL** *has spotted him.)*

THE PRINCE IS GIVING A BALL!

CHRISTOPHER. What...?!

LIONEL.

THE PRINCE IS GIVING A BALL!

VILLAGERS.

> THE PRINCE IS GIVING A BALL!
> THE PRINCE IS GIVING A BALL!
> THE PRINCE IS GIVING A BALL!
> THE PRINCE IS GIVING A BALL!

LIONEL.

> HIS ROYAL HIGHNESS, CHRISTOPHER RUPERT
> WINDEMERE VLADIMIR KARL ALEXANDER
> FRANÇÖIS REGINALD LANCELOT HERMAN...

KIDS.

> HERMAN?

LIONEL.

> ...*HERMAN* GREGORY JAMES,
> IS GIVING A BALL!

VILLAGERS.

> HE'S GIVING A BALL!
> HE'S GIVING A BALL!
> HE'S GIVING A BALL!
> THE PRINCE IS GIVING A BALL!

> (**CINDERELLA** *has been standing off to the side, taking in the excitement.* **LIONEL** *tosses a stack of fliers to the* **VILLAGERS**, *who scramble for them, obscuring* **CINDERELLA**. **LIONEL** *steps down to* **CHRISTOPHER**.)

CHRISTOPHER. (*Approaching* **LIONEL**.) Let me see one of those.

LIONEL. Well, imagine running into you here.

CHRISTOPHER. You're not gonna tell my mom, are you?

LIONEL. You know I got your back, Your Highness.

> (*Handing him a flier.*)

Read it and weep.

CHRISTOPHER. (*Reading.*) "Every eligible young maiden in the kingdom is hereby commanded to attend for introduction to the prince?" Lionel, what's this all about?

LIONEL. Do I look like the social director?

CHRISTOPHER. Of course – I should have known. This has my mother written all over it!

(*He storms off.*)

VILLAGERS.

THE PRINCE IS GIVING A BALL!
THE PRINCE IS GIVING A BALL!
THE PRINCE IS GIVING A BALL!

LIONEL.

HIS ROYAL HIGHNESS, CHRISTOPHER RUPERT,
SON OF HER MAJESTY, QUEEN CONSTANTINA
CHARLOTTE ERMINTRUDE GWENYVERE MAISIE...

KIDS.

MAISIE?

LIONEL.

...*MAISIE* MARGUERITE ANNE
IS GIVING A BALL!

(*The* **STEPMOTHER, GRACE,** *and* **JOY** *enter. The* **STEPMOTHER** *sees* **LIONEL** *and stops in her tracks with a shriek.*)

STEPMOTHER. Aaahhh! The royal steward! What news does he bring?

(*A* **VILLAGER** *hands the* **STEPMOTHER** *a flier.*)

FOUR VILLAGE WOMEN.

THEY'VE SPREAD THE NEWS FROM FAR AND WIDE.

STEPMOTHER. (*Reading the flier excitedly.*)

THE PRINCE IS GIVING A BALL!

FOUR VILLAGE WOMEN.

THEY SAY HE WANTS TO FIND A BRIDE.

STEPMOTHER. (*To her* **DAUGHTERS.**)

HE MAY FIND ONE AT THE BALL!

GRACE.

IF ONLY HE'D PROPOSE TO ME!

JOY.

WHY SHOULDN'T HE PROPOSE TO ME?

STEPMOTHER.
> JUST LEAVE THE HAIR AND CLOTHES TO ME!

ALL.
> THE PRINCE IS GIVING A BALL!

STEPMOTHER. Cinderella, hurry home with those packages.
> I want that salmon on ice before it stinks.

CINDERELLA. Yes, Stepmother.

> *(She exits as* **LIONEL** *approaches the* **CLOTH MERCHANT**.*)*

LIONEL.
> NOW IF YOU PLEASE,
> THEIR MAJESTIES
> REQUEST YOUR FINEST SILK.

CLOTH MERCHANT.
> MY BEST BROCADE
> IN EVERY SHADE!

LIONEL.
> AND LACE AS WHITE AS MILK

OLDER SISTER.
> I'LL WEAR A GOWN
> OF SATIN JADE

YOUNGER SISTER.
> AND ME I'M IN A
> PINK BROCADE

YOUNG GIRL.
> AND ME, I'M IN
> THE SEVENTH GRADE

> *(***LIONEL** *approaches the* **BUTCHER**.*)*

LIONEL.
> SURELY I'LL NEED A SIDE OF HAM
> AND LOTS OF BEEF FILETS.

BUTCHER.
> MARBLEIZED STEAKS, A RACK OF LAMB!

LIONEL.
> AND VEAL YOU RAISE TO BRAISE.

A GIRL.

I WISH I DIDN'T LIKE TO EAT

ANOTHER GIRL.

I WISH I WERE DEMURE AND SWEET

(**LIONEL** *approaches the* **CHEESE MERCHANT.**)

LIONEL.

LIMBURGER CHEESE AND GOURMANDISE.

CHEESE MERCHANT.

CHEDDAR, GRUYERE AND BLEU!

LIONEL.

CHUNKS OF SWISS IN BARRELS, PLEASE.

MAKE SURE THAT IT'S HOLEY, TOO!

(*He approaches the* **BAKER.**)

PUDDING AND PIES AND RUM SOUFFLÉ,

SUCCULENT CHOCOLATE ROUNDS.

BAKER.

CRÈME PUFFS YOU CAN CHEW AWAY!

LIONEL.

TO GAIN SOME ROYAL POUNDS.

ALL.

THE PRINCE IS GIVING A BALL!

THE PRINCE IS GIVING A BALL!

(*The music surges, and the* **VILLAGERS** *kick up their heels in celebration of this exciting news.*)

VILLAGERS.

HIS ROYAL HIGHNESS...

LIONEL.

TWO HUNDRED ORCHIDS, FOUR HUNDRED POPPIES,

SIX HUNDRED ROSES, EIGHT HUNDRED LILLIES...

VILLAGERS.

CHRISTOPHER RUPERT...

LIONEL.

ONE THOUSAND ORANGES, TWO THOUSAND PLUMS...

VILLAGERS.

WINDEMERE VLADIMIR KARL ALEXANDER...

LIONEL.

RASPBERRY, BLUEBERRY, STRAWBERRY, GOOSEBERRY...

VILLAGERS.

FRANÇÖIS REGINALD LANCELOT HERMAN...

LIONEL.

SON OF HER MAJESTY, QUEEN UPSIDE-DOWN CAKE.
CHOCOLATE AND CHEDDAR AND CHARLOTTE AND
    MAISIE.
SON OF HIS CAVIAR, KING MAXIMILLIAN
GODFREY LADISLAUS LEOPOLD SIDNEY...

KIDS.

SIDNEY?

ALL.

SIDNEY!

LIONEL.

...FREDERICK JOHN,
IS GIVING A BALL!

VILLAGERS.

INSIDE THE ROYAL HALL!
THE PRINCE IS GIVING A BALL!

LIONEL.

COME ONE, COME ALL!

VILLAGERS.

HE'S GIVING A BALL!
HE'S GIVING A BALL!
THE PRINCE,
THE PRINCE IS GIVING A BALL!

(Applause segues into:)

[MUSIC NO. 03A "PLAYOFF (THE PRINCE IS GIVING A BALL)"]

(The scene shifts to:)

Scene Two
The Stepmother's Manor House

(Immediately following. **CINDERELLA** *is cleaning the hearth as the* **DOVE** *flies on and perches in the tree. The* **STEPMOTHER, GRACE,** *and* **JOY** *enter in high spirits, leaving the door wide open. The* **STEPMOTHER** *carries a flier announcing the ball.)*

STEPMOTHER, GRACE & JOY. *(A cappella.)* "The prince is giving a ball! The prince is giving a ball! They've spread the news from far and wide, the prince is giving a..."

STEPMOTHER. Cinderella, you let the fire go out. It's cold enough to hang meat in here!

JOY. Well, close the door, Cinderella – duh!

*(**CINDERELLA** crosses and closes the door.)*

STEPMOTHER. *(To* **GRACE** *and* **JOY.***)* Now you listen and you listen good. We have exactly one week until the ball and I do not intend to waste this opportunity. You two will be the loveliest, most well-spoken and vivacious maidens at that ball if it's the last thing I do! Am I understood?

GRACE & JOY. Yes, Mother.

STEPMOTHER. Good. Just imagine – the prince asking for my daughter's hand in marriage!

GRACE. *(Leering at* **JOY.***)* Which daughter is that, I wonder.

JOY. I'm younger and more appealing.

(The door creaks open.)

GRACE. The oldest marries first.

JOY. That's an old wives' tale!

GRACE. Why do you think there's so many old wives runnin' around!

STEPMOTHER. Girls, don't start!

JOY. Mother, Cinderella simply refuses to close that door!

CINDERELLA. But I...

STEPMOTHER. Hold your tongue and do as you're told! Now once and for all, close that door!

(*Again* **CINDERELLA** *closes the door.*)

GRACE. Have you ever seen a lazier girl in your life?

JOY. Who *you* callin' lazy?

GRACE. You want a piece o' me?!

STEPMOTHER. Enough already! Now sit, my daughters – we need to have a talk.

(**GRACE** *and* **JOY** *sit on the sofa;* **CINDERELLA** *also moves to sit.*)

Not you. I want to talk to my *real* daughters. You tend that fire and serve us tea.

CINDERELLA. Yes, Stepmother.

(*She starts for the fireplace.*)

GRACE. I want some crumpets with my tea!

JOY. Like I don't? Crumpets, Cinderella!

CINDERELLA. Coming right up.

(*The dialogue continues as* **CINDERELLA** *goes about stoking the fire.*)

STEPMOTHER. My darlings – I cannot stress strongly enough how imperative it is that you make a proper impression upon the prince. You know, I will not be around forever to care for you.

JOY. Why not?

GRACE. Yeah. Where are *you* goin'?

STEPMOTHER. What I mean to say is that I do not intend to spend the rest of my life slaving away in this house.

(*Shouting across the room.*)

Cinderella, the tea!

(**CINDERELLA** *exits to the kitchen.*)

I have devoted my entire life to your comfort and well-being. Is it asking too much that I spend my golden years in a cottage by the sea?

JOY. And leave us here?

GRACE. Alone?

STEPMOTHER. *(Exasperated.)* Not alone! With *hus-bands*!

> (**CINDERELLA** *enters and hangs the tea kettle over the fire.*)

You know, it takes a certain amount of income to maintain our lifestyle. The funds your stepfather left will not last forever and money does not grow on trees.

> (**CINDERELLA** *exits to the kitchen.*)

GRACE. *(With know-it-all superiority.)* I know that. It comes from the bank.

STEPMOTHER. And how do you suppose it gets into the bank?

JOY. The banker goes and gets it from...well, wherever it *does* grow but not on trees.

STEPMOTHER. Money doesn't grow anywhere! It's inherited! Which is precisely why I am determined to see each of you marry within the year. So either you make a proper impression upon the prince, or it's back to the butcher and Master Boxhorn! Am I understood?

GRACE & JOY. Yes, Mother.

STEPMOTHER. Good. Just imagine – *me*! The mother of a princess! Now come along, girls – enough excitement for one day. It's time for your beauty rest and, Lord knows, you can use it.

> (**CINDERELLA** *enters with the tea service and crumpets, not noticing as the door creaks open.*)

CINDERELLA. Here you go – fresh-baked crumpets and...

STEPMOTHER. *(Impatiently.)* Not now, Cinderella – we're going to nap. Have dinner prepared when we awake. Smoke the salmon.

GRACE. *(Exiting.)* Bake the bread!

JOY. *(Exiting.)* Poach the pears!

STEPMOTHER. And Cinderella – close that door!

(*She exits.* **CINDERELLA** *crosses and closes the door. The kettle in the fireplace whistles, and she races over and takes it off the fire, then sits in the chair by the hearth, with a sigh.*)

CINDERELLA. Ah... Alone at last.

[MUSIC NO. 04 "IN MY OWN LITTLE CORNER"]

(*A* **WHITE MOUSE** *peeks out.*)

It's all right – the coast is clear.

(*Three more* **WHITE MICE** *pop into view, chattering.*)

Sh-h-h, quiet – they're resting.

(*The* **MICE** *scurry over to* **CINDERELLA**. *A cat –* **CHARLES** *– appears.*)

Charles, will you be joining us?

(**CHARLES** *trots across the room and joins the others.*)

I have a surprise.

(*The* **ANIMALS** *lean in eagerly. The* **DOVE** *coos at the window, getting* **CINDERELLA***'s attention.*)

Yes, for you too.

(*The* **DOVE** *disappears momentarily, then re-enters onto the hearth as* **CINDERELLA** *reaches into her pocket.*)

Crumpets, if you please!

(*Spreading the crumbs on the floor and the hearth for the impatient* **ANIMALS**.)

There's enough for everyone, now share. So, how was your day? Same old – same old, huh? Yeah, me too. "Cinderella, the packages!" "Cinderella, the tea!" "Cinderella, the door!" How can three grown women be so helpless? Well, I suppose that's what I get for letting them walk all over me.

I'M AS MILD AND AS MEEK AS A MOUSE...

*(Aside to the **MICE**.)*

No offense.

WHEN I HEAR A COMMAND, I OBEY.
BUT I KNOW OF A SPOT IN MY HOUSE
WHERE NO ONE CAN STAND IN MY WAY.

IN MY OWN LITTLE CORNER IN MY OWN LITTLE CHAIR,
I CAN BE WHATEVER I WANT TO BE.
ON THE WING OF MY FANCY I CAN FLY ANYWHERE
AND THE WORLD WILL OPEN ITS ARMS TO ME.

I'M A YOUNG NORWEGIAN PRINCESS OR A MILKMAID,
I'M THE GREATEST PRIMA DONNA IN MILAN.
I'M AN HEIRESS WHO HAS ALWAYS HAD HER SILK MADE
BY HER OWN FLOCK OF SILKWORMS IN JAPAN.

I'M A GIRL MEN GO MAD FOR, LOVE'S A GAME I CAN PLAY
WITH A COOL AND CONFIDENT KIND OF AIR,
JUST AS LONG AS I STAY IN MY OWN LITTLE CORNER,
ALL ALONE IN MY OWN LITTLE CHAIR.

*(The **ANIMALS** take part as **CINDERELLA** plays out her fantasies.)*

I CAN BE WHATEVER I WANT TO BE.
I'M A THIEF IN CALCUTTA, I'M A QUEEN IN PERU,
I'M A MERMAID DANCING UPON THE SEA.

I'M A HUNTRESS ON AN AFRICAN SAFARI.
IT'S A DANGEROUS TYPE OF SPORT AND YET IT'S FUN!
IN THE NIGHT I SALLY FORTH TO SEEK MY QUARRY
AND I FIND I FORGOT TO BRING MY GUN!

I AM LOST IN THE JUNGLE, ALL ALONE AND UNARMED
WHEN I MEET A LIONESS IN HER LAIR!
THEN I'M GLAD TO BE BACK IN MY OWN LITTLE CORNER,
ALL ALONE IN MY OWN LITTLE CHAIR.

*(The music continues under. The **DOVE** picks up the flier from where it was left and takes it to **CINDERELLA** as the other **ANIMALS** gather around her excitedly.)*

CINDERELLA. Why...? Oh, you want me to read it to you?

> *(The* **ANIMALS** *indicate that they do.)*

Okay. "Every eligible young maiden in the kingdom is hereby commanded to attend for introduction to the prince."

> *(The* **ANIMALS** *react excitedly.)*

What...?

> *(She looks more closely at the flier; not trusting her own eyes.)*

"Every eligible young maiden..."

> *(Music stops.)*

That means me! I'm going to the ball!

> *(The music resumes,* **CINDERELLA** *and the* **ANIMALS** *overjoyed.)*

I AM IN THE ROYAL PALACE, OF ALL PLACES!
I AM CHATTING WITH THE PRINCE AND KING AND
    QUEEN,
AND THE COLOR ON MY TWO STEPSISTERS' FACES
IS A QUEER SORT OF SOUR-APPLE GREEN!

But wait – I don't have anything to wear.

> *(The* **ANIMALS** *scamper to the chest, the* **MICE** *jumping up and down on it while the* **DOVE** *flutters over them.)*

Why are you...? Of course!

> *(She goes to the chest and opens it. To an orchestral glissando, she pulls out a lovely, simple antique dress.)*

The dress Mother wore the night she met Father. He said she was the most beautiful girl he'd ever seen.

> *(Holding the dress up to herself.)*

Oh...it's wonderful! I'll have to take the hem up a little bit...maybe a blue sash... Oh, it's going to be perfect!

(*She twirls to the music, lost in her dreams of going to the ball.*)

LA – LA LA LA LA LA LA

LA – LA LALA –

LALALA – LA –

LALALALALALA –

(*She curtsies before the mirror, then looks up at her reflection, perhaps realizing for the first time what a pretty girl she is.*)

Oh, how can I wait a whole week?

(*She races to the trunk, retrieves some sewing supplies, sits in her chair, and begins hemming the dress, the* **ANIMALS** *at her feet.*)

I'M THE BELLE OF THE BALL IN MY OWN LITTLE CORNER, ALL ALONE IN MY OWN LITTLE CHAIR.

(*Applause segue into:*)

[MUSIC NO. 04A "SCENE CHANGE TO PALACE"]

(*The scene shifts to:*)

Scene Three
The Royal Parlor

(Immediately following. The QUEEN *sits, sewing a button on the king's trousers. The* KING, *clad in his undergarments, is trying to squeeze into a suit jacket that is too small for him. After a sharp orchestra chord, the* QUEEN *speaks:)*

QUEEN. A fine father you are! You never worry about him.

(A sharp orchestra chord.)

KING. What's wrong with him?

(A sharp orchestra chord.)

QUEEN. He isn't happy.

(She bites off the thread and thrusts the pants at the KING *on two orchestra chords. Music out.)*

KING. Of course he is.

(He struggles to get the pants on.)

QUEEN. If he's happy, why doesn't he get married?

KING. If he's happy, why *should* he get married?

(Trying in vain to button the pants.)

Oh, it's no use trying to get these buttoned. They'll just have to do as-is.

QUEEN. Don't be ridiculous. You look like five pounds of flour in a two-pound sack.

(The KING *takes the pants off.)*

The royal tailor will just have to make you a new suit.

KING. But this suit is in perfect shape!

QUEEN. No one is questioning the shape the suit is in, darling.

*(CHRISTOPHER *comes storming into the room, brandishing the flier.)*

CINDERELLA

21

CHRISTOPHER. Mother, what is the meaning of this?

KING. *(Putting on a dressing gown.)* Doesn't anybody in this house knock?

QUEEN. Darling, we were just talking about you.

KING. Your mother was talking, I was listening.

QUEEN. And where have you been, in that costume?

CHRISTOPHER. Why wasn't I consulted about this ball that *I'm* supposedly giving?

QUEEN. Oh, darn – you found out. It was supposed to be a surprise birthday party. Well, surprise!

CHRISTOPHER. It's three months until my birthday. And since when does a birthday party require the attendance of "every eligible young maiden in the kingdom"?

QUEEN. *(Feigning shock and disbelief.)* What...? Let me...

> *(She snatches the flier and gives it a glance.)*

Well, you know those royal printers – they never get anything right.

CHRISTOPHER. Mom, I want this ball called off immediately.

QUEEN. But, darling, it's impossible to cancel once you've got the ball rolling.

> *(She realizes she has made a joke and howls, but she's the only one.)*

CHRISTOPHER. Well, you can just count me out!

> *(He turns on his heels and starts off.)*

KING. Your Highness!

> *(This in a father's tone of voice that pulls* **CHRISTOPHER** *up short.)*

Look, Chris – we don't want to pressure you, but you do have certain obligations.

QUEEN. What your father is trying to say is that it's time to choose a bride and produce an heir. After all, someday soon this kingdom will be yours.

KING. Not *that* soon.

QUEEN. I long to hear the pitter-patter of little feet on the marble again.

CHRISTOPHER. All I'm asking is to find a bride for myself, in my own time. I guess I have this old-fashioned idea that I want to fall in love before I get married. Like you did.

KING. That's what we want for you too, son.

QUEEN. Of course it is, darling. Well, thank goodness we have *that* all settled. Now, I have prepared a short guest list for your approval.

(*As she unfurls a scroll which stretches not quite across the room:*)

[MUSIC NO. 04B "ROYAL SCROLL"]

(**CHRISTOPHER** *and the* **KING** *wince.*)

CHRISTOPHER. You haven't heard a word I've said!

QUEEN. Family and close friends, darling – terribly intimate.

(**LIONEL** *enters.*)

LIONEL. Your Majesties, Your Highness – if you please. I couldn't help overhearing and I probably shouldn't interfere...

KING, QUEEN & CHRISTOPHER. Probably.

LIONEL. But perhaps we can reach a royal compromise.

QUEEN. Compromise?

KING. What do you think this is – a democracy?

CHRISTOPHER. What sort of a compromise, Lionel?

LIONEL. Let's say you suck it up and go along with the ball.

QUEEN. I'm loving this idea so far.

LIONEL. And if you find the girl of your dreams, great.

(*To the* **QUEEN.**)

But if he doesn't...

CHRISTOPHER. Lionel, you're brilliant! Okay, I'll do it. But if I don't meet the right girl at the ball, you'll let me fall in love in my own time, no matter how long it takes...

QUEEN. But...

CHRISTOPHER. And with no interference. Dad?

KING. Well...it does have a certain logic to it.

QUEEN. Of course, darling. If that's the way you want it, that's the way it shall be.

CHRISTOPHER. Thank you. Both.

KING. You know, son, there's only one way to find the girl of your dreams.

CHRISTOPHER. What's that?

KING. Dumb luck. Let's just hope it runs in the family.

CHRISTOPHER. Love you guys.

(He exits.)

LIONEL. Don't worry, Your Majesties. He'll meet the right girl at the ball. I can just feel it in my bones.

QUEEN. You'll feel it in your bones if he doesn't.

LIONEL. I hear that.

(LIONEL exits.)

QUEEN. Max, suppose he *doesn't* meet the right girl at the ball? What then?

[MUSIC NO. 05 "BOYS AND GIRLS LIKE YOU AND ME"]

(Music begins as the KING gently touches the QUEEN's hand.)

KING. Then he'll meet her somewhere else. Isn't that the way it always happens?

BOYS AND GIRLS LIKE YOU AND ME
WALK BENEATH THE SKIES.
THEY LOVE JUST AS WE LOVE,
WITH THE SAME DREAM IN THEIR EYES.
SONGS AND KINGS AND MANY THINGS
HAVE THEIR DAY AND ARE GONE,
BUT BOYS AND GIRLS LIKE YOU AND ME,
WE GO ON AND ON.

QUEEN.

> THEY WALK ON EVERY VILLAGE STREET,
> THEY WALK IN LANES WHERE BRANCHES MEET,
> AND STARS SEND DOWN THEIR BLESSINGS FROM THE
>   BLUE.
> THEY GO THROUGH STORMS OF DOUBT AND FEAR,
> AND SO THEY GO FROM YEAR TO YEAR,
> BELIEVING IN EACH OTHER AS WE DO.

QUEEN & KING.

> BRAVELY MARCHING FORWARD TWO BY TWO.
>
> BOYS AND GIRLS LIKE YOU AND ME
> WALK BENEATH THE SKIES.
> THEY LOVE JUST AS WE LOVE,
> WITH THE SAME DREAM IN THEIR EYES.
> SONGS AND KINGS AND MANY THINGS
> HAVE THEIR DAY AND ARE GONE,
> BUT BOYS AND GIRLS LIKE YOU AND ME,
> WE GO ON AND ON.

> *(The scene shifts to:)*

Scene Three A
A Palace Corridor

(Immediately following. **CHRISTOPHER** *enters, followed by* **LIONEL.***)*

LIONEL. So tell me, why did you disappear again this morning after I've begged you...

CHRISTOPHER. I had a remarkable day! No one treated me like a prince. I was just a normal person.

LIONEL. You know what? Normal people? Not all they're cracked up to be. *I'm* a normal person. Doesn't that tell you anything? They're all out there wishing they could be *you.*

CHRISTOPHER. Because they don't know what it's really like.

LIONEL. Look – you're rich, you live in a gorgeous palace, you've got every woman in the kingdom throwing herself at you. Is there something I'm not getting?

CHRISTOPHER. I have no life of my own. Everything gets decided for me. You should know that better than anyone, always hanging over me like a cloud, everywhere I go, everything I do. I mean – get a life.

LIONEL. I got a life and it's you! I'm your royal steward and I'm telling you – this disappearing act has got to stop. It's too dangerous.

CHRISTOPHER. I was careful.

LIONEL. Not you – me! I can't keep lying to your mother about where you are. They got laws against that. Now what say we slip into something less comfortable.

(He helps **CHRISTOPHER** *into a robe.)*

[MUSIC NO. 06 "THE SWEETEST SOUNDS (REPRISE)"]

(The scene begins to shift.)

CHRISTOPHER.
THE MOST ENTRANCING SIGHT OF ALL
IS YET FOR ME TO SEE,

AND THE DEAREST LOVE IN ALL THE WORLD
IS WAITING SOMEWHERE FOR ME –
IS WAITING SOMEWHERE...

> (**CINDERELLA** *has appeared at the hearth, holding her mother's dress. They sing in a round.*)

CHRISTOPHER & CINDERELLA.

THE SWEETEST SOUNDS I'LL EVER HEAR
ARE STILL INSIDE MY HEAD.
THE KINDEST WORDS I'LL EVER KNOW
ARE WAITING TO BE SAID.

THE MOST ENTRANCING SIGHT OF ALL
IS YET FOR ME TO SEE...

CINDERELLA.

AND THE DEAREST LOVE IN ALL THE WORLD
IS WAITING SOMEWHERE FOR ME –

CHRISTOPHER.

WAITING SOMEWHERE,

CINDERELLA.

WAITING SOMEWHERE...

CHRISTOPHER.

WAITING SOMEWHERE...

> (*He exits.*)

> (*The scene has now shifted to:*)

Scene Four
The Manor House

(One week later. **CINDERELLA** *exits as the* **STEPMOTHER, JOY,** *and* **GRACE** *enter, all decked out for the ball. Music out.)*

STEPMOTHER. Tonight my girls will be the envy of everyone at the ball!

JOY. Do you really think so, Mother?

GRACE. She said so, didn't she?

STEPMOTHER. Why, our family has always been known for its fascinating women. I might have married a prince myself if I'd had the advantages you've had.

(With growing bitterness.)

If I'd had someone to push me like you girls do, someone to sacrifice everything for *me*!

(She collects herself.)

Now tell me, Grace – what will you say when you meet the prince?

*(***GRACE** *is a bundle of nerves, anxious for her mother's approval, and when she's nervous, she itches uncontrollably.)*

GRACE. Well, you said to show him there's more to me than mere beauty, so I'm going to recite a poem.

JOY. Poetry? Bor-ing!

GRACE. Is not!

JOY. Is so!

GRACE. Not!

JOY. So!

GRACE. *Not!*

STEPMOTHER. *So* much bickering, so little time! For heaven's sake, Grace, stop scratching yourself.

GRACE. I can't help it. You know I get itchy when I'm nervous.

STEPMOTHER. Poppycock! Now Joy, how do you plan to make an impression upon the prince?

JOY. I've been cultivating my naturally infectious laughter.

GRACE. As if.

JOY. The prince's every witty remark will be met with peals of delighted laughter.

> *(She demonstrates, topping off her high-pitched twitter with an involuntary snort.)*

STEPMOTHER. *(Wincing.)* Joy, I beg of you, whatever you do – do not snort at the prince. Remember girls: "The clever bride hides her flaws..."?

JOY & GRACE. "...Until *after* the wedding."

STEPMOTHER. Good!

CINDERELLA. *(Entering, wearing her mother's dress.)* So, what do you think?

STEPMOTHER. Think about what, Cinderella?

CINDERELLA. *(Turning to show off her dress.)* My dress. For the ball.

STEPMOTHER. The ball? You?

> *(They look to one another, then break into fits of laughter.)*

CINDERELLA. What's so funny? Every eligible girl is *commanded* to attend.

STEPMOTHER. I'll do the commanding around here! So, tell me, Lady Cinderella, what would you say to capture the prince?

CINDERELLA. I won't try to capture him. I'll get to know him – ask him about himself.

STEPMOTHER. Fascinating. Take my advice, Cinderella, which I give with all my heart. Know your place and be satisfied with it. And your place is here.

GRACE. You were gonna go to the royal palace in that funky old thing?

JOY. Now *that's* funny!

(*She lets rip with a series of giggles and snorts.*)

STEPMOTHER. Now, girls, there's no need to be mean.

(*Crossing to* **CINDERELLA**, *slyly.*)

Cinderella, I think your dress is...sweet. It becomes you. It's just that, well –

(*She grabs the sleeve, gives it a yank, and rips the dress, which now hangs sadly.*)

Cheap cloth, Cinderella. Like what you're cut from.

CINDERELLA. (*Struggling to control herself.*) This was my mother's dress and it's beautiful.

STEPMOTHER. Your mother was common and so is that dress. And so are you.

CINDERELLA. If my father were alive...

STEPMOTHER. But he's not, is he?

CINDERELLA. I have as much right to go to the ball as they do!

STEPMOTHER. Right? You have a right?! When your father died everyone said, "Throw her into the street! After all, she's not *your* daughter!" But no. I've kept you on all these years – sacrificed for you at the expense of my *own* daughters! And this is the thanks I get!

GRACE. Have you ever seen a more ungrateful child in your life?

JOY. Who are *you* callin' ungrateful?!

GRACE. (*Ready to slug her.*) Sister, you are workin' my last good nerve!

STEPMOTHER. Now girls, I do not want you getting upset. Be a swan, Grace, be a swan.

(**GRACE** *breathes deeply and flutters her arms a bit.*)

Shoulders back, Joy, and try to live up to your name.

(**JOY** *smiles lamely. We hear the carriage pulling up outside the house.*)

STEPMOTHER. Ah, there's the coach. Girls, this is our big chance – don't fail me now. And remember: "Restraint…"?

GRACE & JOY. "…Above all else!"

STEPMOTHER. Good! Cinderella, the door.

> *(There's a moment when, for the first time, we're not certain **CINDERELLA** will obey. But finally she crosses slowly, opens the door, and her **STEPMOTHER** and **STEPSISTERS** parade out.)*

(Offstage.) To the palace and make it snappy!

> *(**CINDERELLA** stands watching as the carriage rolls off into the distance without her. She closes the door and hurries to her chair by the fireplace. The door creaks open and all she can do is bury her face in her hands.)*

[MUSIC NO. 07 "IN MY OWN LITTLE CORNER (REPRISE)"]

> *(The **MICE** come out of hiding, go to the door, and with some effort, push it shut. **CHARLES** and the **DOVE** appear, and the **ANIMALS** all go to **CINDERELLA**, who takes off her mother's dress and puts on her raggedy dress as she sings sadly.)*

I AM STANDING BY HIS HIGHNESS OF ALL PLACES,
AND WE FACE THE COURT MAGNIFICENTLY CLOTHED,
I'M THE ENVY OF A THOUSAND STARING FACES
WHO HAVE JUST HEARD THAT I AM HIS BETROTHED.

> *(She lovingly folds her mother's dress and replaces it in the chest.)*

I'M THE BELLE OF THE BALL IN MY OWN LITTLE CORNER,
ALL ALONE…

> *(No longer able to hold back her emotions, **CINDERELLA** breaks down crying, as the scene has shifted to:)*

Scene Five
The Pumpkin Patch Behind the Manor House

(Immediately following. Music continues under. The tree we have seen in the distance outside the manor house is now downstage and, from this new perspective, enormous. **CINDERELLA** *kneels beneath the tree. The* **ANIMALS** *enter and look on sympathetically.)*

CINDERELLA. I don't know what to do, Mother. I try so hard to win their affection but nothing I do is right. Why do they hate me so much? What's wrong with me? Oh, I wish... I wish I could go to the ball – I do! I wish it with all my heart!

(The music swells to the roll of thunder and flashes of lightning. The **FAIRY GODMOTHER** *seems to materialize from within the tree. Music out.)*

Who are you?

FAIRY GODMOTHER. I'm your Fairy Godmother, honey.

CINDERELLA. You?

FAIRY GODMOTHER. Do you have a problem with that?

CINDERELLA. No! I mean... It's just that I always thought...

FAIRY GODMOTHER. Let me guess. A tutu and a magic wand?

CINDERELLA. Well...yeah, sort of.

FAIRY GODMOTHER. Been there, done that.

CINDERELLA. May I ask you something?

FAIRY GODMOTHER. Within reason.

CINDERELLA. Why have you come? Is it because you heard my wish?

FAIRY GODMOTHER. Wishes?

[MUSIC NO. 08 "FOL-DE-ROL"]

FOL-DE-ROL AND FIDDLEDY DEE,
FIDDELDY FADDLEDY FODDLE,
ALL THE WISHES IN THE WORLD
ARE POPPYCOCK AND TWADDLE!

CINDERELLA. You don't really believe that, do you? That wishes are poppycock?

FAIRY GODMOTHER. Why shouldn't I?

CINDERELLA. Well, whenever I dream of having a fairy godmother...

FAIRY GODMOTHER. Dreams?
> FOL-DE-ROL AND FIDDLEDY DEE,
> FIDDELDY FADDLEDY FOODLE,
> ALL THE DREAMERS IN THE WORLD
> ARE DIZZY IN THE NOODLE.

CINDERELLA. So, my wishes are poppycock and I'm crazy for dreaming.

   (*Aside, to the* **ANIMALS.**)

With a fairy godmother like that, who needs a stepmother?

FAIRY GODMOTHER. You know what her problem is? She can't handle how fabulous you are.

CINDERELLA. Fabulous? *Me?*

FAIRY GODMOTHER. Those girls of hers can't hold a candle to you and they all know it. Jealousy! That's why they treat you as they do.

CINDERELLA. But they're my family. They're all I've got.

FAIRY GODMOTHER. Believe me, honey – when your daddy remarried, this is not what he had in mind for you.

CINDERELLA. You talk like you knew him.

FAIRY GODMOTHER. I did know him.

CINDERELLA. And Mother?

FAIRY GODMOTHER. Very well.

CINDERELLA. Was she...my mother, I mean – was she beautiful?

FAIRY GODMOTHER. Well, people did seem to think so. But your mama never put much stock in beauty. The way you look isn't really something you can take credit or blame for, is it?

CINDERELLA. I wish I'd known her.

FAIRY GODMOTHER. So does she, honey.

CINDERELLA. I've wished so hard...

FAIRY GODMOTHER. Wishes again! Look – it is true that everything *starts* with a wish. But it is what you *do* with a wish that counts.

[MUSIC NO. 09 "IMPOSSIBLE"]

CINDERELLA. So my wish to go to the ball?

FAIRY GODMOTHER. Fol-de-rol and fiddledy dee. How would you get there? I suppose one of those pumpkins is going to magically transform into a golden carriage.

CINDERELLA. Well, no...

FAIRY GODMOTHER. And that those mice will somehow become horses to pull your magic carriage.

CINDERELLA. Of course not. That's impossible.

FAIRY GODMOTHER. If you say so.

IMPOSSIBLE
FOR A PLAIN YELLOW PUMPKIN TO BECOME A GOLDEN CARRIAGE.
IMPOSSIBLE
FOR A PLAIN COUNTRY BUMPKIN AND A PRINCE TO JOIN IN MARRIAGE.
AND FOUR WHITE MICE WILL NEVER BE FOUR WHITE HORSES.
SUCH FOL-DE-ROL AND FIDDLEDY DEE OF COURSE IS IMPOSSIBLE!

BUT THE WORLD IS FULL OF ZANIES AND FOOLS
WHO DON'T BELIEVE IN SENSIBLE RULES
AND WON'T BELIEVE WHAT SENSIBLE PEOPLE SAY,
AND BECAUSE THESE DAFT AND DEWY-EYED DOPES
KEEP BUILDING UP IMPOSSIBLE HOPES,
IMPOSSIBLE THINGS ARE HAPPENING EVERY DAY!

IMPOSSIBLE.

CINDERELLA.
IMPOSSIBLE?

FAIRY GODMOTHER.
IMPOSSIBLE.

CINDERELLA.

IMPOSSIBLE?

FAIRY GODMOTHER.

IMPOSSIBLE!

CINDERELLA.

IMPOSSIBLE!

CINDERELLA & FAIRY GODMOTHER.

IMPOSSIBLE!

CINDERELLA. But wait!

> *(The music continues under.)*

If impossible things are happening every day, then why not my impossible wish?

> *(She kneels and gives it her all, as if pleading with the universe itself.)*

I wish I could go to that ball tonight more than anything in the world! I wish it for every girl who ever wanted to go to a dance and was told she couldn't. And I wish that all the kind hearts in the universe would put their heads together and...

FAIRY GODMOTHER. The kind *hearts* would put their *heads* together?

CINDERELLA. You know what I mean. I just want every good soul to hear my wish and know that I'm ready to do everything I can to make it come true.

FAIRY GODMOTHER.

IMPOSSIBLE
FOR A PLAIN YELLOW PUMPKIN TO BECOME A GOLDEN
    CARRIAGE.
IMPOSSIBLE

CINDERELLA. But wait...

FAIRY GODMOTHER.

FOR A PLAIN COUNTRY BUMPKIN AND A PRINCE TO JOIN
    IN MARRIAGE.
AND FOUR WHITE MICE WILL NEVER BE TURNED TO
    HORSES.

CINDERELLA. Why not!

FAIRY GODMOTHER.
> SUCH FOL-DE-ROL AND FIDDLEDY DEE OF COURSE IS
> IMPOSSIBLE!

CINDERELLA.
> BUT THE WORLD IS FULL OF ZANIES AND FOOLS.

FAIRY GODMOTHER.
> IMPOSSIBLE.

CINDERELLA.
> WHO DON'T BELIEVE IN SENSIBLE RULES.

FAIRY GODMOTHER.
> IMPOSSIBLE!

CINDERELLA.
> AND WON'T BELIEVE WHAT SENSIBLE PEOPLE SAY.

FAIRY GODMOTHER.
> FOL-DE-ROL AND FIDDLEDY DEE!

CINDERELLA.
> AND BECAUSE THESE DAFT AND DEWY-EYED DOPES
> KEEP BUILDING UP IMPOSSIBLE HOPES,

CINDERELLA & FAIRY GODMOTHER.
> IMPOSSIBLE THINGS ARE HAPPENING EVERY...

> *(Music continues under.)*

You know what? If I really wanted to go to that ball badly enough, nothing could stop me.

FAIRY GODMOTHER. You know what? You're right.

CINDERELLA. There are bound to be carriages going by. I can catch a ride with one of them!

FAIRY GODMOTHER. Of course you can.

CINDERELLA. And I can fix that dress in nothing flat! Thanks!

> *(She races off.)*

FAIRY GODMOTHER. Cinderella, wait!

CINDERELLA. *(Re-entering.)* Yes?

FAIRY GODMOTHER. Now that you're ready to take responsibility for your own destiny –

(The music segues into:)

[MUSIC NO. 09A "THE TRANSFORMATION"]

(The **FAIRY GODMOTHER** *gestures toward a pumpkin as the music becomes increasingly mysterioso. The pumpkin begins rocking, then rolls itself to center stage. She turns her attention to the* **ANIMALS**, *and as if bewitched, they move into position next to the pumpkin, creating a tableau. The music crescendos, and a sudden storm of fog, wind, and light sends* **CINDERELLA** *back several steps. She watches in awe as the pumpkin is magically transformed into an opulent golden carriage. The* **MICE** *become* **WHITE HORSES;** **CHARLES** *is transformed into a* **COACHMAN,** *seated decorously at the reins of the carriage; the* **DOVE** *is transformed into a* **FOOTMAN,** *standing attendant on the running board at the rear of the carriage. As the music sustains, the* **FAIRY GODMOTHER** *then turns to* **CINDERELLA**.*)*

FAIRY GODMOTHER. Now, about that dress –

[MUSIC NO. 10 "IT'S POSSIBLE: FINALE ACT I"]

(Again the music swells. The **FAIRY GODMOTHER** *gives* **CINDERELLA** *a spin;* **CINDERELLA** *spins upstage and around the carriage, emerging in a dazzling gown and beautiful evening slippers made of glass. The music holds a tremolo while she considers herself and the glass slippers, barely able to believe her eyes. At last she sings:)*

CINDERELLA.
IT'S POSSIBLE!

CINDERELLA.	HORSES, COACHMAN & FOOTMAN.
FOR A PLAIN YELLOW PUMPKIN TO BE-	OO... OH...
COME A GOLDEN CARRIAGE.	AH... CARRIAGE.
IT'S POSSIBLE	IT'S POSSIBLE
FOR A PLAIN COUNTRY BUMPKIN AND A	OO... OH...
PRINCE TO JOIN IN MARRIAGE.	AH... MARRIAGE

(As they continue, the **FOOTMAN** *helps* **CINDERELLA** *and the* **FAIRY GODMOTHER** *into the carriage.)*

AND FOUR WHITE MICE ARE	OH...
EASILY TURNED TO HORSES!	HORSES!

CINDERELLA & FAIRY GODMOTHER.

SUCH FOL-DE-ROL AND FIDDLEDY DEE	AH...
OF COURSE IS...	OF COURSE IS

CINDERELLA.

...QUITE POSSIBLE!

FAIRY GODMOTHER. To the palace, Charles!

(The carriage embarks upon its journey as the scene begins to shift.)

CINDERELLA & FAIRY GODMOTHER.

FOR THE WORLD IS FULL OF ZANIES AND FOOLS

HORSES, COACHMAN & FOOTMAN.

IT'S POSSIBLE!

CINDERELLA & FAIRY GODMOTHER.

WHO DON'T BELIEVE IN SENSIBLE RULES

HORSES, COACHMAN & FOOTMAN.

QUITE POSSIBLE!

CINDERELLA & FAIRY GODMOTHER.

AND WON'T BELIEVE WHAT SENSIBLE PEOPLE SAY.

ALL.

AND BECAUSE...

CINDERELLA & FAIRY GODMOTHER.

...THESE DAFT AND DEWY-EYED DOPES...

ALL.

...KEEP BUILDING...

CINDERELLA & FAIRY GODMOTHER.

...UP IMPOSSIBLE HOPES...

ALL.

...IMPOSSIBLE THINGS ARE HAPPENING EVERY...

CINDERELLA & FAIRY GODMOTHER.

...DAY!

HORSES, COACHMAN & FOOTMAN.

THEY'RE HAPPENING EVERY DAY,

IMPOSSIBLE THINGS ARE HAPPENING EVERY DAY!

*(The music continues, gradually slowing with
the clip-clop of the* **HORSES** *as they arrive:)*

Scene Six
Outside The Royal Palace

FAIRY GODMOTHER.

IT'S POSSIBLE.

CINDERELLA.

IT'S POSSIBLE.

HORSES, COACHMAN & FOOTMAN.

IT'S POSSIBLE.

CINDERELLA.

IT'S POSSIBLE.

FAIRY GODMOTHER, HORSES, COACHMAN & FOOTMAN.

IT'S POSSIBLE.

CINDERELLA.

IT'S POSSIBLE.

ALL.

IT'S POSSIBLE!

> *(The* **FOOTMAN** *opens the door of the carriage and helps* **CINDERELLA** *and the* **FAIRY GODMOTHER** *out.* **CINDERELLA** *is overwhelmed at the sight of the palace, and increasingly nervous.)*

FAIRY GODMOTHER. Well, have a lovely night.

> *(She turns to go.)*

CINDERELLA. But aren't you coming in?

FAIRY GODMOTHER. Honey, I've done so many of these dos, I couldn't do another do.

CINDERELLA. But I'm afraid.

FAIRY GODMOTHER. Of what?

CINDERELLA. That I won't fit in. You know – with the other girls.

FAIRY GODMOTHER. I was never big on fitting in. I always preferred to stand out.

CINDERELLA. But nothing in my life has prepared me for a night like this.

FAIRY GODMOTHER. And yet everything in your life has led you to this moment. Look around, Cinderella – your wish has been granted. Now get in there and do something with it.

CINDERELLA. Thank you – for everything.

(They embrace, and **CINDERELLA** *turns toward the palace steps.)*

FAIRY GODMOTHER. Oh, Cinderella – just one thing more. Extremely important. You must leave the palace before the clock strikes twelve.

CINDERELLA. Before midnight? But all the girls get to stay out late tonight.

FAIRY GODMOTHER. Not you.

CINDERELLA. But...

FAIRY GODMOTHER. No more buts. Just make certain you leave before midnight.

CINDERELLA. Okay – I will.

(The **FAIRY GODMOTHER** *watches as* **CINDERELLA** *starts tentatively toward the palace steps, insecure and self-conscious.)*

FAIRY GODMOTHER. And Cinderella?

(The music pauses.)

You're as beautiful tonight as your mother ever was.

(The music resumes; **CINDERELLA** *holds herself tall, beaming with a new sense of confidence.)*

FAIRY GODMOTHER, HORSES, COACHMAN & FOOTMAN.
IMPOSSIBLE THINGS ARE HAPPENING EVERY DAY!

*(***CINDERELLA** *proceeds regally up the palace steps as the curtain falls.)*

ACT II

[MUSIC NO. 11 "ENTR'ACTE"]

(The music segues into:)

[MUSIC NO. 12 "GAVOTTE"]

Scene One
The Royal Ballroom

*(The curtain rises on a stately gavotte, the mood stiff and deadly dull. The **KING** and **QUEEN** sit to one side on their thrones as **LIONEL** attends to a line of* **MAIDENS***. The **STEPMOTHER**, **GRACE**, and **JOY** enter grandly. In a seemingly endless succession, **CHRISTOPHER** dances with each **MAIDEN** in turn.)*

QUEEN. Have you ever seen so many lovely girls?

KING. It looks like Chris is having a worse time than I am.

QUEEN. Oh, darling, he'll find the one he's looking for tonight.

KING. And if he doesn't?

QUEEN. It's going to be a long night.

*(The **STEPMOTHER** approaches **LIONEL**.)*

STEPMOTHER. Pardon me, Your Stewardship, but I'm sure you've noticed my two beautiful daughters.

*(**GRACE** and **JOY** bat their eyelashes and give **LIONEL** a little wave as the **STEPMOTHER** pulls a monetary note from her bosom and presses it into **LIONEL**'s palm.)*

LIONEL. *(Refusing the money.)* Please, madam – His Highness will dance with all the young ladies in due course.

STEPMOTHER. *(Flirtatiously.)* Naturally, every mother is eager that her daughter should dance with the prince. But what I want to know is, who has the honor of dancing with his steward?

LIONEL. Stewards don't dance.

STEPMOTHER. Now, there's no need to be coy.

> *(All over him.)*

There's a look in your eye that says...

LIONEL. Please don't touch.

STEPMOTHER. Let's not pretend, Lionel. I can sense a certain something between us.

LIONEL. I wish there was something between us. A continent.

> *(CHRISTOPHER signals surreptitiously to LIONEL that he's had enough of his MAIDEN partner. LIONEL, in an effort to rid himself of the STEPMOTHER, escorts JOY over to CHRISTOPHER. CHRISTOPHER bows to the MAIDEN and turns to dance with JOY, who immediately begins to giggle.)*

CHRISTOPHER. Have I missed something?

> *(JOY rings forth peals of nervous laughter and snorts.)*

What's so funny?

JOY. Your Highness is so witty!

CHRISTOPHER. How would you know? I haven't said anything yet.

> *(Again the STEPMOTHER corners LIONEL.)*

STEPMOTHER. So tell me, Lionel, when a girl marries a prince, she becomes a royal princess?

LIONEL. Yep.

STEPMOTHER. Which would make her mother a royal...

LIONEL. Pain in the neck.

(**JOY** *positively roars with both laughter and snorts;* **CHRISTOPHER** *gives* **LIONEL** *the signal.* **LIONEL** *escorts* **GRACE** *to* **CHRISTOPHER** *as he bows to* **JOY**, *who is now in hysterics.* **LIONEL** *leads* **JOY** *back to the* **STEPMOTHER**.)

CHRISTOPHER. Good evening.

GRACE. Hi, there.

(*She's already getting itchy.*)

"Ships that pass in the night and speak to each other in passing on the ocean of life."

CHRISTOPHER. Excuse me?

GRACE. That's poetry.

CHRISTOPHER. Oh. Do you have a rash?

GRACE. Why would you ask that?

CHRISTOPHER. Because you're scratching yourself.

GRACE. (*More and more frantic.*) "Ships that pass in the night." That's like you and me.

CHRISTOPHER. Is it?

(*He signals* **LIONEL**, *who crosses to him.*)

GRACE. "On the ocean of life!" That's like, you know – water!

CHRISTOPHER. Thank you, miss, for the distinct pleasure of your company.

(**LIONEL** *leads the scratching* **GRACE** *back to the anxious* **STEPMOTHER** *as* **CHRISTOPHER** *crosses to the* **KING** *and* **QUEEN**.)

How much more of this are you going to put me through?

QUEEN. Why, darling, it's the shank of the evening!

(**LIONEL** *approaches* **CHRISTOPHER**.)

LIONEL. So, ready for the next round?

CHRISTOPHER. I suppose so. The sooner I get through 'em all, the sooner I can get out of here.

KING. That's the spirit.

> *(The gavotte continues,* **CHRISTOPHER** *dancing with* **MAIDENS** *one after another. With his staff,* **LIONEL** *stamps each change of partner, the tempo increasing with each new partner, as the dance becomes more and more frenzied.* **CHRISTOPHER**, *however, seems to be lost in a world only he can see. The music segues directly into:)*

[MUSIC NO. 13 "LONELINESS OF EVENING"]

CHRISTOPHER.

I WAKE IN THE LONELINESS OF SUNRISE
WHEN THE DEEP PURPLE HEAVEN TURNS BLUE,
AND START TO PRAY,
AS I PRAY EACH DAY,
THAT I'LL HEAR SOME WORD FROM YOU.

I LIE IN THE LONELINESS OF EVENING
LOOKING OUT ON A SILVER-FLAKED SEA,
AND ASK THE MOON,
"OH, HOW SOON, HOW SOON,
WILL MY LOVE APPEAR TO ME?"
WILL MY LOVE APPEAR...

> *(The music segues into:)*

[MUSIC NO. 14 "THE CINDERELLA ENTRANCE AND WALTZ"]

> *(Without warning,* **CINDERELLA** *appears at the top of the staircase.* **CHRISTOPHER** *looks up at this radiant vision and seems frozen in place. One by one, the* **GUESTS** *follow* **CHRISTOPHER**'s *gaze toward* **CINDERELLA**, *everyone falling silent. As* **CINDERELLA** *descends the staircase,* **CHRISTOPHER**, *like a man in a trance, crosses to meet her at the foot of the stairs. The music pauses as* **CHRISTOPHER** *speaks.)*

> *(Extending his hand.)*

May I have the pleasure of this dance?

CINDERELLA. *(Taking his hand, with a curtsy.)* I'd be delighted, Your Highness.

> *(The music moves into "The Cinderella Waltz Theme.")*
>
> *(**CHRISTOPHER** and **CINDERELLA** glide onto the dance floor as everyone watches intently. The **GUESTS** join them and are soon caught up in the lush waltz. After the dance climaxes, the music becomes softer as the **KING** speaks, during which the dance continues.)*

KING. Well, things are lookin' up!

QUEEN. Lionel, who is that captivating creature?

LIONEL. Beats me. No one seems to know. But she sure looks fine.

QUEEN. Hmmm. Shall we join them, Your Majesty?

KING. I'd be honored, Your Majesty.

> *(The **KING** escorts the **QUEEN** onto the dance floor, and they join in the waltz as **CINDERELLA** and **CHRISTOPHER** dance into view. The music segues into:)*

[MUSIC NO. 15 "TEN MINUTES AGO"]

CHRISTOPHER. Forgive me, but haven't we met before?

CINDERELLA. No, Your Highness.

CHRISTOPHER. You're certain?

CINDERELLA. I think I'd remember meeting a prince.

CHRISTOPHER. *(Chuckling bashfully.)* Yeah, I guess so. Have you ever met someone and felt as if you'd known them forever?

CINDERELLA. Not until tonight.

CHRISTOPHER.
TEN MINUTES AGO I SAW YOU.
I LOOKED UP WHEN YOU CAME THROUGH THE DOOR.
MY HEAD STARTED REELING,
YOU GAVE ME THE FEELING
THE ROOM HAD NO CEILING OR FLOOR.

TEN MINUTES AGO I MET YOU,
AND WE MURMURED OUR HOW-DO-YOU-DOS.
I WANTED TO RING OUT THE BELLS AND FLING OUT
MY ARMS AND TO SING OUT THE NEWS.

I HAVE FOUND HER!
SHE'S AN ANGEL
WITH THE DUST OF THE STARS IN HER EYES!
WE ARE DANCING,
WE ARE FLYING
AND SHE'S TAKING ME BACK TO THE SKIES.

IN THE ARMS OF MY LOVE I'M FLYING
OVER MOUNTAIN AND MEADOW AND GLEN,
AND I LIKE IT SO WELL
THAT FOR ALL I CAN TELL
I MAY NEVER COME DOWN AGAIN!
I MAY NEVER COME DOWN TO EARTH AGAIN!

> (*The music continues under as the* **KING**
> *and* **QUEEN** *dance up to* **CHRISTOPHER** *and*
> **CINDERELLA**.)

KING. (*Tapping* **CHRISTOPHER** *on the shoulder.*) May I?

CHRISTOPHER. Dad...

> (*Before he can object, the* **KING** *dances away*
> *with* **CINDERELLA**, *and the* **QUEEN** *sweeps*
> **CHRISTOPHER** *into her arms for a dance.*)

Mom...

QUEEN. Darling, who is that enchanting girl?

CHRISTOPHER. That's what I was trying to find out when we
were so rudely interrupted.

QUEEN. Of course it doesn't really matter. You told me
yourself you wouldn't find the girl of your dreams
tonight.

CHRISTOPHER. Maybe I was wrong.

QUEEN. But more importantly...?

CHRISTOPHER. Okay, I admit it. You were right!

I HAVE FOUND HER!
SHE'S AN ANGEL
WITH THE DUST OF THE STARS IN HER EYES!
WE ARE DANCING,
WE ARE FLYING
AND SHE'S TAKING ME BACK TO THE SKIES.

> *(They dance away as* **CINDERELLA** *and the* **KING** *dance into view.)*

KING. I don't believe we've seen you before. Do we know your parents?

CINDERELLA. I don't think so.

KING. Well then, you must introduce us.

CINDERELLA. Well, my father... And my mother, well... she... I'm sorry, Your Majesty. Will you excuse me for a moment?

KING. Of course, my dear.

> *(***CINDERELLA** *curtsies and hurries away as the* **QUEEN** *and* **CHRISTOPHER** *dance into view.)*

CHRISTOPHER. Thank you, Your Majesty.

QUEEN. *(With a proper curtsy.)* Charmed, Your Highness.

> *(***CHRISTOPHER** *turns to look for* **CINDERELLA** *and unexpectedly finds himself dancing with the* **FAIRY GODMOTHER**, *who has suddenly appeared out of the crowd.)*

FAIRY GODMOTHER. I couldn't help noticing that divine girl you were dancing with.

CHRISTOPHER. That's my mother.

FAIRY GODMOTHER. Not her. I mean the girl who's leaving.

CHRISTOPHER. Leaving...?

> *(He sees* **CINDERELLA** *heading up the staircase.)*

Will you excuse me?

> *(He hurries to* **CINDERELLA**.*)*

You're not leaving already?

CINDERELLA. Well I...

CHRISTOPHER. Look, I don't know what my dad said to you but...

CINDERELLA. Oh, no – he was wonderful.

CHRISTOPHER. Then please – stay for just one more dance? I know we haven't known each other very long, but how do you think it's going?

> *(He extends his hand to her.* **CINDERELLA** *can't resist, and he leads her onto the dance floor, and she sings.)*

CINDERELLA.

> TEN MINUTES AGO I MET YOU,
> AND WE MURMURED OUR HOW-DO-YOU-DOS.
> I WANTED TO RING OUT
> THE BELLS AND FLING OUT
> MY ARMS AND TO SING OUT THE NEWS.
>
> I HAVE FOUND HIM! I HAVE FOUND HIM!
> HE'S THE LIGHT OF THE STARS IN MY EYES
> WE ARE DANCING
> WE ARE FLYING
> AND HE'S TAKING ME BACK TO THE SKIES!

> *(***CHRISTOPHER** *and* **CINDERELLA** *are joined by other waltzing* **COUPLES** *as they sing.)*

COMPANY.

> IN THE ARMS OF MY LOVE I'M FLYING
> OVER MOUNTAIN AND MEADOW AND GLEN,
> AND I LIKE IT SO WELL
> THAT FOR ALL I CAN TELL
> I MAY NEVER COME DOWN AGAIN!
> I MAY NEVER COME DOWN TO EARTH AGAIN!

> *(The music soars, the room is awhirl with waltzing* **COUPLES.***)*
>
> *(Applause segue into:)*

Scene Two
The Royal Gardens

[MUSIC NO. 15A "PLAYOFF POLKA AND UNDERSCORE"]

(Immediately following. As the COUNTES *polka offstage to another part of the palace,* CHRISTOPHER *strolls downstage with* CINDERELLA *as the scene begins to shift. A full moon illuminates a beautiful garden, which includes statuary, a bench, and upstage topiary.)*

CHRISTOPHER. May I ask you something?

CINDERELLA. Within reason.

CHRISTOPHER. What brought you here tonight?

CINDERELLA. Well, it's kind of a long story. My family didn't want me to come. In fact, they don't even know I'm here.

CHRISTOPHER. I'm glad you are.

(The others are gradually fading upstage and off.)

The truth is I almost didn't come myself.

CINDERELLA. How could a prince not show up for his own ball?

CHRISTOPHER. Don't you think it's all a little...medieval? I guess it's no secret that my folks are anxious to marry me off. You know – being heir to the throne and all. But this whole thing makes me feel like some kind of a...a prized bull or something.

CINDERELLA. *(Teasing him, playing the femme fatale.)* Every eligible young maiden vying to be your devoted servant, forever and forever?

CHRISTOPHER. Servants I got. What I need is...someone I can really talk to.

(They share a look of understanding.)

(Music has concluded.)

CINDERELLA. It's beautiful out here.

CHRISTOPHER. *(Never taking his eyes off her.)* Yes, it is.

> *(He tries drawing close to her, but she turns away nervously.)*

You're not like most girls, are you?

CINDERELLA. Not like the girls you meet, I suppose.

CHRISTOPHER. Actually, I don't meet that many girls. I lead a pretty sheltered life.

CINDERELLA. So do I.

CHRISTOPHER. Really? Every day, same old – same old?

CINDERELLA. Having no life of your own...

CHRISTOPHER. ...The same silly arguments...

CINDERELLA. ...Until you just want to run away...

CINDERELLA & CHRISTOPHER. ...And never come back!

> *(They laugh at having completed each other's thought.)*

CHRISTOPHER. It seems like we have a lot in common.

CINDERELLA. Oh... I'm not so sure about that. After all, you don't really know me.

CHRISTOPHER. But I'd like to. And I want you to know me.

> *(Taking her hands.)*

Look, I know we've just met and it's crazy and everything but...

> *(He looks deep into her eyes...then chickens out.)*

Would you like to see the rest of the gardens?

CINDERELLA. I'd love to.

[MUSIC NO. 16 "STEPSISTERS' LAMENT"]

> *(An orchestral sting, and* **JOY** *peeks out from behind a topiary, unseen by* **CHRISTOPHER** *and* **CINDERELLA**, *as they stroll off romantically.)*

JOY. Did you get a good look at her?

(Another sting, and **GRACE** *peeks out from behind another topiary.)*

GRACE. Only a glance.

*(***JOY*** and* **GRACE** *hurry downstage.)*

Could you hear what they were saying?

JOY. Only a word or two.

GRACE. She must be a princess or something.

JOY. His Highness sure seemed to go for her.

GRACE. Well, there's just no accounting for taste.
WHY WOULD A FELLOW WANT A GIRL LIKE HER,
A FRAIL AND FLUFFY BEAUTY?
WHY CAN'T A FELLOW EVER ONCE PREFER
A SOLID GIRL LIKE ME?

JOY.
SHE'S A FROTHY LITTLE BUBBLE
WITH A FLIMSY KIND OF CHARM,
AND WITH VERY LITTLE TROUBLE
I COULD BREAK HER LITTLE ARM!

GRACE.
OH!

JOY.
OH!

JOY & GRACE.
WHY WOULD A FELLOW WANT A GIRL LIKE HER,
SO OBVIOUSLY UNUSUAL?
WHY CAN'T A FELLOW EVER ONCE PREFER
A USUAL GIRL LIKE ME?

GRACE.
HER FACE IS EXQUISITE, I SUPPOSE.

JOY.
BUT NO MORE EXQUISITE THAN A ROSE IS.

GRACE.
HER SKIN MAY BE DELICATE AND SOFT.

JOY.
BUT NOT ANY SOFTER THAN A DOE'S IS.

GRACE.

HER NECK IS NO LONGER THAN A SWAN'S.

JOY.

SHE'S ONLY AS DAINTY AS A DAISY.

GRACE.

SHE'S ONLY AS GRACEFUL AS A BIRD.

JOY & GRACE.

SO WHY IS THE FELLOW GOING CRAZY?

OH, WHY WOULD A FELLOW WANT A GIRL LIKE HER,
A GIRL WHO'S MERELY LOVELY?
WHY CAN'T A FELLOW EVER ONCE PREFER
A GIRL WHO'S MERELY ME?

JOY.

SHE'S A FROTHY LITTLE BUBBLE
WITH A FRILLY SORT OF AIR

GRACE.

AND WITH VERY LITTLE TROUBLE
I COULD PULL OUT ALL HER HAIR!

JOY & GRACE.

OH! OH!
WHY WOULD A FELLOW WANT A GIRL LIKE HER,
A GIRL WHO'S MERELY LOVELY?
WHY CAN'T A FELLOW EVER ONCE PREFER
A GIRL WHO'S MERELY ME?

WHAT'S THE MATTER WITH THE MAN?
WHAT'S THE MATTER WITH THE MAN?
WHAT'S THE MATTER WITH THE MAN?

> (*The* **STEPSISTERS** *stomp off. Applause segue as* **CINDERELLA** *and* **CHRISTOPHER** *return from their walk.*)

[MUSIC NO. 17 "DO I LOVE YOU BECAUSE YOU'RE BEAUTIFUL?"]

CHRISTOPHER. So even when it's just the three of us, we eat every meal at a table that seats forty-two people. It's insane.

CINDERELLA. I must say, you certainly lead an interesting life.

CHRISTOPHER. It's become a lot more interesting tonight. Isn't it strange how things happen? A girl I've never seen before comes down a flight of stairs and suddenly nothing will ever be the same.

CINDERELLA. Do you believe in guardian angels?

CHRISTOPHER. Guardian angels?

CINDERELLA. You know – someone who watches over you, kind of helping things along. Maybe someone from a long time ago you thought went away but who never really left at all. Do you believe in such things?

CHRISTOPHER. Does that explain why you're the most entrancing sight I'll ever see? Why your voice is the sweetest sound I'll ever hear? Does it explain why I think I've fallen in love with you?

DO I LOVE YOU BECAUSE YOU'RE BEAUTIFUL,
OR ARE YOU BEAUTIFUL BECAUSE I LOVE YOU?
AM I MAKING BELIEVE I SEE IN YOU
A GIRL TOO LOVELY TO BE REALLY TRUE?

DO I WANT YOU BECAUSE YOU'RE WONDERFUL,
OR ARE YOU WONDERFUL BECAUSE I WANT YOU?
ARE YOU THE SWEET INVENTION OF A LOVER'S DREAM,
OR ARE YOU REALLY AS BEAUTIFUL AS YOU SEEM?

> (**CINDERELLA** *turns away, and* **CHRISTOPHER** *senses he's gone too far.*)

I guess it's not a very good sign when you tell someone you love them and they don't say anything.

CINDERELLA. I'm afraid that if I speak, I might wake up.

CHRISTOPHER. Are you dreaming that I'm about to kiss you?

> (*The music soars as* **CHRISTOPHER** *takes* **CINDERELLA** *into his arms, and they kiss.*)

CINDERELLA.
AM I MAKING BELIEVE I SEE IN YOU
A MAN TOO PERFECT TO BE REALLY TRUE?

DO I WANT YOU BECAUSE YOU'RE WONDERFUL,
OR ARE YOU WONDERFUL BECAUSE I WANT YOU?

CHRISTOPHER.

I WANT YOU!

CHRISTOPHER & CINDERELLA.

ARE YOU THE SWEET INVENTION OF A LOVER'S DREAM,

CHRISTOPHER.

OR ARE YOU

CHRISTOPHER.	**CINDERELLA.**
REALLY AS WONDERFUL	ARE YOU AS WONDERFUL
AS YOU SEEM?	AS YOU SEEM?

CHRISTOPHER & CINDERELLA.

ARE YOU REALLY AS WONDERFUL AS YOU...

(The music segues into:)

[MUSIC NO. 18 "TWELVE O'CLOCK"]

(The moon suddenly becomes the face of a clock at the stroke of midnight as chimes begin ringing out and the scene begins to shift.)

CINDERELLA. *(Horrified.)* No...!

(She bolts from the gardens and exits to the ballroom.)

CHRISTOPHER. Wait...please... Don't go!

*(He runs off after her; the scene has shifted to the ballroom. **CINDERELLA** runs through and exits up the staircase. The scene has now shifted to:)*

Scene Three
Outside The Royal Palace

(Immediately following. Music continues under. CINDERELLA, again in her raggedy dress, runs down the steps of the palace. CHARLES and the MICE are waiting next to the pumpkin upstage, on which the DOVE is perched – the same tableau they formed prior to their transformations. CINDERELLA takes one look back at the palace as she and the ANIMALS hurry off. CHRISTOPHER enters and rushes down the steps, looking off in both directions. The KING, QUEEN, and LIONEL hurry on.)

KING. What happened, Chris?

QUEEN. What did you say to her, darling?

CHRISTOPHER. I don't know. We were in the gardens and.

LIONEL. What the...?

(Music has concluded. Something sparkling on the steps has caught LIONEL's eye. CHRISTOPHER picks it up.)

CHRISTOPHER. An evening slipper – made of glass. She must've lost it when she ran out. I've got to find her!

LIONEL. What's her name?

CHRISTOPHER. I don't know.

KING. Where does she live?

CHRISTOPHER. I don't know.

QUEEN. Well you certainly didn't get to know her very well.

CHRISTOPHER. I felt like I knew her the moment we met.

KING. But you don't know anything about her.

CHRISTOPHER. I know that she's different than any other girl in the world.

[MUSIC NO. 19 "DO I LOVE YOU BECAUSE YOU'RE BEAUTIFUL? (REPRISE)"]

CHRISTOPHER. All my life I've been searching for something. I didn't know what exactly but I found it tonight – in her.

KING. How can you be so sure?

CHRISTOPHER.

DO I LOVE HER BECAUSE SHE'S BEAUTIFUL?

KING.

OR IS SHE BEAUTIFUL BECAUSE YOU LOVE HER?

CHRISTOPHER.

AM I MAKING BELIEVE I SEE IN HER

A GIRL TOO LOVELY TO BE REALLY TRUE?

DO I WANT HER BECAUSE SHE'S WONDERFUL?

QUEEN.

OR IS SHE WONDERFUL BECAUSE YOU WANT HER?

CHRISTOPHER. I can't lose her – not now.

KING. It's all right, son. She's out there somewhere.

CHRISTOPHER. Lionel, we're going to search for the foot that fits this slipper. We'll try it on every girl in the kingdom if we have to!

(He hands **LIONEL** *the slipper.)*

LIONEL. Who dances in glass shoes? Ouch!

CHRISTOPHER. We'll leave at dawn. Have the stable master prepare the coach.

LIONEL. Consider it done, Your Highness. By the way, am I the only one who's noticed that pumpkin sitting there?

(They all turn upstage and look at the pumpkin for the first time.)

QUEEN. *(Crossing up the stairs to the palace.)* Do take it to the pantry, Lionel, before someone trips over it.

LIONEL. A glass shoe and a pumpkin. What a night.

(He exits.)

KING. Chris – we'll find her.

>   *(He exits with the **QUEEN** as the scene begins to shift.)*

CHRISTOPHER.
>   AM I MAKING BELIEVE I SEE IN YOU
>   A GIRL TOO PERFECT TO BE REALLY TRUE?
>   DO I WANT YOU BECAUSE YOU'RE WONDERFUL,
>   OR ARE YOU WONDERFUL BECAUSE I WANT YOU?

>   *(**CINDERELLA** appears.)*

CHRISTOPHER & CINDERELLA.
>   ARE YOU THE SWEET INVENTION OF A LOVER'S DREAM,
>   OR ARE YOU REALLY AS WONDERFUL AS YOU SEEM?

>   *(The scene has now shifted to:)*

Scene Four
The Manor House

(Later that night. The **STEPMOTHER, GRACE,** *and* **JOY** *are lounging about, regaling* **CINDERELLA** *with a not entirely truthful account of their evening;* **CINDERELLA** *is serving tea.)*

STEPMOTHER. ...But when the king got up and led the orchestra with a loaf of French bread – well, laugh? I thought I'd die!

(Music out.)

GRACE. Word up, the best night of my life!

JOY. *Your* life?

CINDERELLA. Did you get to dance with the prince?

GRACE. I only danced with him for an hour or so.

JOY. An hour?!

GRACE. Why? Didn't you?

JOY. Of course I did, if *you* did.

STEPMOTHER. I wouldn't be the least bit surprised if the prince chose one of my girls for his bride.

CINDERELLA. It sounds almost too good to be true. Did you know everyone?

STEPMOTHER. Everyone who's anyone.

GRACE. Except for some Princess Something-or-other who arrived late and left early.

CINDERELLA. A princess?

[MUSIC NO. 20 "WHEN YOU'RE DRIVING THROUGH THE MOONLIGHT"]

Did she dance with the prince?

STEPMOTHER. I didn't notice.

CINDERELLA. Do you think he liked her?

GRACE. What's with all the questions?

JOY. Really! I feel positively interrogated!

CINDERELLA. I'm sorry. I'm just trying to imagine what it must have been like.
> WHEN YOU'RE DRIVING THROUGH THE MOONLIGHT ON THE HIGHWAY,
> WHEN YOU'RE DRIVING THROUGH THE MOONLIGHT TO THE DANCE,
> YOU ARE BREATHLESS WITH A WILD ANTICIPATION
> OF ADVENTURE AND EXCITEMENT AND ROMANCE.
>
> THEN AT LAST YOU SEE THE TOWERS OF THE PALACE
> SILHOUETTED ON THE SKY ABOVE THE PARK,
> AND BELOW THEM IS A ROW OF LIGHTED WINDOWS,
> LIKE A LOVELY DIAMOND NECKLACE IN THE DARK.

GRACE.
> IT LOOKS THAT WAY.

JOY.
> THE WAY YOU SAY.

STEPMOTHER.
> SHE TALKS AS IF SHE KNOWS.

CINDERELLA.
> I DO NOT KNOW
> THESE THINGS ARE SO –
> I ONLY JUST SUPPOSE.
>
> I SUPPOSE THAT WHEN YOU COME INTO THE BALLROOM
> AND THE ROOM ITSELF IS FLOATING IN THE AIR,
> IF YOU'RE SUDDENLY CONFRONTED BY HIS HIGHNESS,
> YOU ARE FROZEN LIKE A STATUE ON THE STAIR.
>
> YOU'RE AFRAID HE'LL HEAR THE WAY YOUR HEART IS BEATING,
> AND YOU KNOW YOU MUSTN'T MAKE THE FIRST ADVANCE.
> YOU ARE SERIOUSLY THINKING OF RETREATING,
> THEN YOU SEEM TO HEAR HIM ASKING YOU TO DANCE,

JOY, GRACE & STEPMOTHER.	**CINDERELLA.**
HE IS TALL...	AND STRAIGHT AS A LANCE!
AND HIS HAIR...	IS DARK AND WAVY.

JOY, GRACE & STEPMOTHER.   **CINDERELLA.**
   HIS EYES...   CAN MELT YOU WITH A
                                        GLANCE!

JOY, GRACE & STEPMOTHER.
   HE CAN TURN A GIRL TO GRAVY!

     (The music continues as underscoring.)

GRACE. And when you waltz, he whirls you around so that
   your feet never touch the floor.

JOY. And you can feel his hot breath on your neck.

STEPMOTHER. *(Shivering at the thought.)* Oo-oo...

     (The music segues into:)

[MUSIC NO. 21 "A LOVELY NIGHT"]

CINDERELLA.

   A LOVELY NIGHT, A LOVELY NIGHT –
   A FINER NIGHT YOU KNOW YOU'LL NEVER SEE.
   YOU MEET YOUR PRINCE, A CHARMING PRINCE –
   AS CHARMING AS A PRINCE WILL EVER BE!

   THE STARS IN A HAZY HEAVEN
   TREMBLE ABOVE YOU
   WHILE HE IS WHISPERING,
   "DARLING, I LOVE YOU."

     (The others are increasingly drawn in by
     CINDERELLA*'s story.)*

   YOU SAY GOOD-BYE,
   AWAY YOU FLY,
   BUT ON YOUR LIPS YOU KEEP A KISS.
   ALL YOUR LIFE YOU'LL DREAM OF THIS
   LOVELY, LOVELY NIGHT.

     (The **STEPFAMILY** *have momentarily forgotten*
     their disdain for **CINDERELLA***, so caught up*
     are they in her romantic vision. They prance
     about, acting out their fantasies of having
     charmed the prince themselves. The **ANIMALS**
     eventually become involved in the number,
     but remain unseen until later when the
     STEPFAMILY *sees a mouse.)*

GRACE.

A LOVELY NIGHT.

JOY.

A LOVELY NIGHT.

STEPMOTHER, GRACE & JOY.

A FINER NIGHT YOU KNOW YOU'LL NEVER SEE.

GRACE.

YOU MEET YOUR PRINCE.

JOY.

A CHARMING PRINCE.

STEPMOTHER, GRACE & JOY.

AS CHARMING AS A PRINCE WILL EVER BE!

CINDERELLA.

THE STARS IN A HAZY HEAVEN...

CINDERELLA, GRACE & JOY.

...TREMBLE ABOVE YOU...

CINDERELLA.

...WHILE HE IS WHISPERING,

STEPMOTHER.

"DARLING, I LOVE YOU."

ALL.

YOU SAY GOOD-BYE,

AWAY YOU FLY,

BUT ON YOUR LIPS YOU KEEP A KISS.

ALL YOUR LIFE YOU DREAM OF THIS

LOVELY, LOVELY NIGHT.

> (*The* **ANIMALS** *suddenly appear, unseen by the others.*)
>
> (*From, this point on, the* **ANIMAL** *voices can be covered offstage by women in chipmunk voices.*)

ANIMALS.

LA LA LA LA LA LA LA LA,

LA LA LA LA LA LA LA!

STEPFAMILY. (*Seeing a* **MOUSE.**) Aaahhh!

> *(As they resume singing, a lively dance ensues,*
> *everyone having a good, silly time of it.)*

ALL.

YOU SAY GOOD-BYE,
AWAY YOU FLY.

CINDERELLA.

BUT ON YOUR LIPS YOU KEEP A KISS.

ALL.

ALL YOUR LIFE YOU'LL DREAM OF THIS

CINDERELLA.

LOVELY

GRACE.

LOVELY

JOY.

LOVELY

CINDERELLA, GRACE, JOY & STEPMOTHER.

LOVELY NIGHT!

ANIMALS.

LOVELY NIGHT!

ALL.

LOVELY NIGHT!

> *(The number has concluded. They* **ALL** *laugh*
> *together, delighted by their impromptu*
> *performance, truly enjoying each other's*
> *company. The* **STEPMOTHER** *suddenly becomes*
> *conscious of the free-wheeling behavior and*
> *pulls herself up imperiously.)*

STEPMOTHER. Nonsense! Rubbish and drivel!

> *(***GRACE*** and* **JOY** *think they've been addressed.)*

JOY. Yes...?

GRACE. Yes...?

STEPMOTHER. It was nothing like that! And the two of
you, hanging on her every word! Enough! Go to your
rooms – it's late.

(GRACE and JOY exit, and the STEPMOTHER turns her attentions to CINDERELLA.)

And as for you, princess – get your head out of the clouds! Your father spoiled you rotten with a lot of empty dreams and impossible wishes that will never come true! You're a little fool, Cinderella, and I do not suffer fools gladly.

(She exits.)

[MUSIC NO. 22 "A LOVELY NIGHT (REPRISE)"]

(The ANIMALS emerge and scurry to CINDERELLA's side, but she needs no consoling. Even her stepmother's reproach cannot diminish her buoyant spirits tonight!)

CINDERELLA. *(Softly, in memory.)*
THE STARS IN A HAZY HEAVEN
TREMBLING ABOVE ME,
DANCED WHEN HE PROMISED
ALWAYS TO LOVE ME.

THE DAY CAME THROUGH,
AWAY I FLEW,
BUT ON MY LIPS HE LEFT A KISS.
ALL MY LIFE I'LL DREAM OF THIS
LOVELY, LOVELY NIGHT.

(The music segues into:)

Scene Five
Throughout the Kingdom

(The following day and night.)

[MUSIC NO. 23 "THE SEARCH"]

(A drop flies in downstage, depicting a map of the kingdom.)

(Behind the drop, in shadow, in a series of vignettes, we see **CHRISTOPHER** *and* **LIONEL** *trying the slipper on the feet of* **MAIDENS** *throughout the kingdom. As more and more feet appear, growing ever more surreal in size, the search becomes increasingly frantic. The images eventually turn ghoulish as the sequence takes on the qualities of a comic nightmare. At the peak of the madness, the drop flies out to reveal* **CHRISTOPHER** *and* **LIONEL**, *who watch as the* **DOVE** *flies around the stage. As the* **DOVE** *makes its way offstage,* **CHRISTOPHER** *and* **LIONEL** *decided to follow it. The scene shifts to:)*

Scene Six
The Manor House

(The following morning. The music concludes as the **STEPMOTHER**, **GRACE**, *and* **JOY** *are lounging in their bedclothes, soaking their feet and indulging in their various beauty regimen. As they chat,* **CINDERELLA** *cleans out the fireplace. The* **STEPMOTHER** *is reading from a scroll. Music out.)*

STEPMOTHER. Doctor Feelbright, the pharmacist?

GRACE. Too flighty.

STEPMOTHER. Master Greenfield, the grocer?

JOY. Too geeky.

STEPMOTHER. Lord Hedgerow, the horticulturist?

GRACE & JOY. Too hairy!

STEPMOTHER. Girls! Perhaps you are being too particular. I am up to the I's!

GRACE. You want us to be happy, don't you?

STEPMOTHER. Of course I do. Like any mother, I want you to have all the things I never had.

(The doorbell rings.)

Now who in the world could that be, at this hour and unannounced?

*(**CINDERELLA** peers out the window.)*

CINDERELLA. *(Excitedly.)* It's the royal steward!

STEPMOTHER. Aaahhh...!

[MUSIC NO. 23A "MANIC STEPSISTERS UNDERSCORE"]

He can't see me like this! Cinderella, fetch my boa!

*(Pandemonium ensues as the **STEPMOTHER** and **STEPSISTERS** hustle to make themselves presentable, and **CINDERELLA** scrambles to retrieve their accoutrements.)*

GRACE. My vest, Cinderella!

JOY. Cinderella, my jacket!

GRACE. Why would he be *here*?

STEPMOTHER. He's come to call on me, you dolt! He's obviously smitten!

>*(**GRACE** stubs her toe on a bucket.)*

GRACE. Ouch...!

STEPMOTHER. Cinderella, get these buckets out of here.

JOY. Cinderella! This isn't my jacket!

CINDERELLA. It's inside-out!

>*(She exits with the buckets.)*

JOY. Oh.

GRACE. I think I broke my toe!

JOY. You?! I almost broke my arm getting this jacket on!

>*(The **STEPMOTHER** pulls the flowers from a vase, rips the buds off, and puts the barren stems back in the vase.)*

STEPMOTHER. Cinderella!

>*(**CINDERELLA** comes running on. Music out.)*

Take this vase to the kitchen and stay there until my guest has gone and I come for you. Am I understood?

CINDERELLA. Of course, Stepmother.

>*(She hurries off with the vase as the **STEPMOTHER** shoves the flowers in her hair.)*

STEPMOTHER. All right, girls – a lesson in how to greet a suitor. Watch and learn.

>*(She opens the door with a flourish; **LIONEL** enters, bearing a royal cushion upon which the beautiful glass slipper sits. The **STEPMOTHER** doesn't notice that **CHRISTOPHER** is right behind him.)*

Lionel –

>*(She slams the door in **CHRISTOPHER**'s face.)*

What a pleasant surprise! I just knew there was something special between us.

LIONEL. Have we met?

STEPMOTHER. *(All over him.)* You were obviously intrigued by our little tête-à-tête at the ball.

LIONEL. Madam, please – some restraint.

GRACE & JOY. "Restraint above all else!"

(The STEPMOTHER glares at the STEPSISTERS.)

LIONEL. *(Opening the door.)* Presenting His Royal Highness, Prince Christopher.

(CHRISTOPHER enters, looking exhausted. The STEPMOTHER and STEPSISTERS are simply agog, staring gape-jawed as they execute their awkward curtsies.)

CHRISTOPHER. *(With a half-hearted bow.)* Ladies. I am in search of the maiden whose foot fits that slipper.

LIONEL. She lost it at the ball.

STEPMOTHER. Really...?

(You can practically see the wheels turning.)

Why, I was saying to my lovely daughter, Joy, just this very morning –

(Grabbing JOY's arm.)

– I was saying, "Joy, whatever happened to your other shoe?" Wasn't I, dear?

(JOY, dumbfounded, can only stare at CHRISTOPHER and nod lamely.)

I was saying, "Where could you have lost it?"

(Squeezing JOY's arm.)

Wasn't I, dear?

JOY. Ouch!

(Finally getting it.)

Oh-h-h! That's my shoe!

(She grabs the slipper.)

JOY. I'd know this shoe anywhere!

STEPMOTHER. Of course you would.

> *(**JOY** attempts to cram her foot into the slipper.)*

LIONEL. Sweetheart...?

> *(**JOY** is not taking no for an answer.)*

Joy...? The shoe is made of glass – it doesn't stretch.

> *(He takes the shoe.)*

GRACE. *(Grabbing the slipper from **LIONEL**.)* Why, that's my shoe, sister! You know that!

> *(Sitting in the chair.)*

Here, Your Highness, let me show ya. Fits me like a glove.

> *(She tries shoving her foot into the slipper.)*

Well, it fit me perfectly at the ball. You see, I had a little accident right before you came. I kicked the bucket and my toe is all swollen up. I don't suppose you got that other shoe with ya.

LIONEL. *(Taking the slipper from **GRACE**.)* Are there any other women in the house?

STEPMOTHER. Why, yes – there is one more.

> *(**GRACE** and **JOY** look at her, stunned, thinking she's referring to **CINDERELLA**. The **STEPMOTHER** pulls **GRACE** from the chair.)*

Move it!

> *(She sits and extends her foot toward **LIONEL**.)*

LIONEL. I meant to say *younger* women.

STEPMOTHER. How much younger?

LIONEL. Younger than you.

STEPMOTHER. Oh, please, I'm begging – *please* take one of my daughters! Joy has had charm and elocution –

JOY. "Peter Piper picked his pepper."

STEPMOTHER. She's really much smarter than she looks. And Grace – that's girl's strong as an ox! And cultured? Why, she can recite "The Wreck of the Hesperus" in three languages!

GRACE. Four if you count Pig Latin!

(*Reciting.*) Uh-thay Eck-ray uh-fay uh-thay Esperas-hay eye-bay Illiam-way Oddsworth-way Ongfello-lay.

> (*She continues reciting the poem under* **LIONEL**'*s next line.*)

"It-ay uz-way uh-thay ooner-scay Espems-hay at-thay ailed-say uh-thay intry-way ee-say, an-day uh-thay kipper-say ad-hay aken-tay is-hay ittle-lay aughter-day oo-tay air-bay im-hay umpany-hay."

LIONEL. Look, lady, it's been a long day. So for the last time, are there any other young women in the house?

STEPMOTHER. (*To* **GRACE**.) Oh, will you shut up!

(*To* **LIONEL**.) No – there are no other *young* women in the house.

[MUSIC NO. 23B "THE SLIPPER FITS"]

> (*As* **CHRISTOPHER** *and* **LIONEL** *turn to leave,* **CINDERELLA** *unexpectedly enters from the kitchen.*)

CINDERELLA. I'm here.

STEPMOTHER. What?!

CINDERELLA. I'm sorry, Stepmother, but I *am* here.

STEPMOTHER. A scullery maid!

JOY. A servant girl!

GRACE. A chimney sweep!

LIONEL. Well, you certainly sound like a girl of many talents. What say we try on...?

CHRISTOPHER. Wait a minute. Didn't I "bump" into you in the village about a week ago?

CINDERELLA. In the...? Oh, now I remember! You helped with my packages.

CHRISTOPHER. Yeah, that was right after I knocked 'em out of your arms.

CINDERELLA. You said that everyone deserves to be treated with kindness and respect.

CHRISTOPHER. You never did tell me your name.

CINDERELLA. It's Cinderella.

CHRISTOPHER. What a beautiful name.

> (LIONEL *clears his throat, bringing* CHRISTOPHER'*s attention back to the business at hand.* CHRISTOPHER *takes the slipper from* LIONEL *and turns to* CINDERELLA.)

May I, Cinderella?

> (*The music builds as* CINDERELLA *sits in her chair by the fireplace, and* CHRISTOPHER *gets down on one knee before her.*)

STEPMOTHER. This can't be happening!

> (CINDERELLA *slips her foot into the slipper, and, of course, it's the perfect fit.*)

(*Fainting.*) Ah-h-h-h...!

CHRISTOPHER.

I HAVE FOUND HER!

CINDERELLA.

ARE YOU THE SWEET INVENTION OF A LOVER'S DREAM?

CHRISTOPHER.

I HAVE FOUND HER!

> (*He takes* CINDERELLA *into his arms, and they kiss as the scene shifts to:*)

Scene Seven
The Wedding Finale

(CINDERELLA and CHRISTOPHER exit as the FAIRY GODMOTHER appears. The music segues into:)

[MUSIC NO. 24 "THERE'S MUSIC IN YOU"]

FAIRY GODMOTHER.
SOMEONE WANTS YOU, YOU KNOW WHO.
NOW YOU'RE LIVING, THERE'S MUSIC IN YOU.
NOW YOU'RE HEARING SOMETHING NEW,
SOMEONE'S PLAYING THE MUSIC IN YOU.

(During this song, two trees upstage have created a canopy against a sumptuous sky. As the song continues, the VILLAGERS enter in eager anticipation of the royal wedding; the MICE and CHARLES are present as well. As the singing continues, the KING and QUEEN enter beneath the canopy, the COMPANY bowing and curtsying to them. LIONEL enters with the STEPMOTHER clamped to his arm. CINDERELLA and CHRISTOPHER enter, followed by GRACE and JOY carrying the train of CINDERELLA's wedding dress. As they pass the STEPMOTHER, she curtsies graciously to CINDERELLA, who smiles at her with a warm nod.)

NOW YOU'RE LIVING, YOU KNOW WHY.
NOW THERE'S NOTHING YOU WON'T TRY.

MOVE A MOUNTAIN,
LIGHT THE SKY,
MAKE A WISH COME TRUE.
THERE IS MUSIC IN YOU!

COMPANY.
OOOO...
THERE IS MUSIC...
NOW...

FAIRY GODMOTHER.

NOW YOU CAN GO WHEREVER YOU WANT TO GO!

COMPANY.

YOU CAN GO WHEREVER YOU WANT TO GO!

FAIRY GODMOTHER.

NOW YOU CAN DO WHATEVER YOU WANT TO DO!

COMPANY.

YOU CAN DO WHATEVER YOU WANT TO DO!

FAIRY GODMOTHER.

NOW YOU CAN BE WHATEVER YOU WANT TO BE!

COMPANY.

BELIEVE IN MUSIC AND LOVE.

FAIRY GODMOTHER.

AND LOVE IS THE SONG YOU WILL SING YOUR WHOLE
LIFE THROUGH!

BARITONES.

THERE IS MUSIC IN YOU. IN YOU.

TENORS.

THERE IS MUSIC IN YOU.

ALTOS.

THERE IS MUSIC.

COMPANY.

THERE IS MUSIC.

FAIRY GODMOTHER.	**COMPANY.**
MOVE A MOUNTAIN,	MOVE A MOUNTAIN,
LIGHT THE SKY,	LIGHT THE SKY,

FAIRY GODMOTHER & COMPANY.

MAKE A WISH COME TRUE.
THERE IS MUSIC IN YOU!

(The **DOVE** *flies on and circles* **CINDERELLA**
and **CHRISTOPHER** *as they kiss, then flies to
the* **FAIRY GODMOTHER** *and alights on her
hand as:)*

(The curtain falls.)

[MUSIC NO. 25 "CURTAIN CALL AND EXIT MUSIC"]

The End